Nortia Press is an independent publisher of
fiction and nonfiction books with a global affairs bent.

For a full catalog visit our website: www.NortiaPress.com

REBEL STREETS

A NOVEL OF THE IRISH TROUBLES

REBEL STREETS

Tom Molloy

TOM MOLLOY

NORTIA
PRESS

ange County, California

www.nortiapress.com

2321 E 4th Street, C-219
Santa Ana, CA 92705
contact @ nortiapress.com

Author photo by Rita Molloy

Library of Congress Control Number: 2012942444
ISBN: 9780984835911

1. Political conflict—Northern Ireland—Fiction
2. Belfast (Northern Ireland)—Fiction
3. Terrorism—Northern Ireland—Fiction
4. Great Britain—History—20th century—Fiction

Printed in the United States

For the people of the Lower Falls.

In particular for Jim and Lillian McEwan, for their unwavering generosity, humor, and courage.

The hood pressed Jimmy's face as he thought—*this breath, this breath, God give me this breath, God let me breathe*. Again the fist hit the side of the hood, Jimmy's knees giving out as strong arms embraced him, holding him upright for the next round of beating. Beneath the hood was stale air, cold blood, the bright faces of his past, all mixed and mocking as he tried to cry out to God, to his mother, to nothing, as now they shook him.

He caught a glimpse of his bare feet off the ground. *How strong these men are* he thought as they shook him, *so strong*. When they stopped shaking him they let him fall as his mind told him, *I could sleep now, if they lift me I could sleep against their strength*.

He saw shoes perfectly black and shiny. The shoes squeaked as the policeman wearing them pulled the prisoner close to say,

"You're going to die now, Jimmy."

He released Jimmy, who fell face down on the floor where they pinned his arms back, lifting him by his hair and ankles, making every injury scream. He saw the back of the black shoes as he cried out, the hood coming into his mouth, trying to suffocate him, the black cloth like something alive all wet and curling to smother him.

They ran, twisting him, he screamed at the running feet of the policemen and they were running and still inside the building, running and this was the worst pain of all, it came from within his brain, lighting every trace of the pain and focused it and he screamed until they dropped him on the wooden floor.

Then silence as his heart pounded, panicking against his chest, seeking to flee this place. *Please God one breath.* Then the gentle voice came to him and a man's hands came under the hood and lifted his face very gently.

"Jimmy lad, I don't want you to die."

Who is this kind stranger? Jimmy's tears met the hands and the man signaled his love and understanding, his fingers gently massaging Jimmy's cheeks.

"I know, Jimmy, I know."

Then they pulled him from the floor, arms pinned back and they ran again, around and around. They ran so long their short breaths felt warm against the black hood. All the while Jimmy was screaming and suffocating and this is when the barrier between his body and the world vanished. He was carried and carried, then dropped.

There was darkness and the gentle caress of the kind strong man returned and he said, "Jimmy, Jimmy, Jimmy."

Jimmy wept and the fingers against his face told him they understood. Then the fingers held him in pure love and the voice asked,

"Jimmy, where is the safe house?"

The prisoner blinked at the tears and pressed his cheek to the kind hands. He tried to say a prayer, to explain, to embrace this other human being amid the white pain but then grunted and shook his head no.

The hands went away. He braced for the kicks, for the curses. He had been trained. Picture the flame of a single candle. Think of that flame and nothing else. Think of nothing else and you will get through. Others have done it. You can do it. The simple beautiful flame of a single lovely candle.

Jimmy heard the sound of a helicopter landing outside and the loving hands came back.

"Jimmy, that's the army. They're going to put you in that machine and go to one thousand feet and throw you out. Jimmy a thousand foot fall. How long will that take?"

Footsteps came, a group of them, the steady footfalls of soldiers who stood all around the crumpled man beneath the hood.

"Jimmy, please. Where is the safe house?"

Jimmy saw no candle, felt only the suffocation and his pounding heart. Then he grunted and shook his head no.

The soldiers carried him down the hall, he felt cool night air, felt the ugly presence of the machine and he was inside the helicopter.

It leapt up, pressing him to the metal floor, up, he could feel the cold, up, up toward God as he tried to pray, *I am heartily sorry, sorry.* He could remember nothing else of any prayer, then *Hail Mary, full of grace.*

The cold permeated him, pulled his skin away to reveal everything that could feel pain beneath. He shook violently with terror and the damp cold. *It will hurt all at once but just for a moment, the fall, how will I endure the fall? Trust to God. Trust to God.*

"Over target area, Sir, altitude one thousand."

The machine vibrated in anticipation as Jimmy thought, *God forgive me, forgive me.*

Then the hands were back to his face, the policeman's lips close to his ear, close and warm as a lover's.

"Jimmy, these men are killers. Jimmy please, for your family, where is the safe house?"

The policeman felt the change in position of the prisoner, the deep exhalation, and pulled closer, wishing the information from the man.

"I love Ireland," gasped the prisoner.

"Goodbye Jimmy."

The soldiers took his wrists and ankles.

"One," said the English voice as they swung him.

God forgive me, God forgive me, forgive, forgive.

"Two."

Now they adjusted their grips for a better hold. Jimmy saw the candle, saw it, then lost it.

"Three."

Jimmy sailed, he could feel the change from the air inside to the atmosphere outside and the rotor's ferocious air blast hit him and he sailed.

His bladder and sphincter loosened and he felt that warmth, and he sailed, and everything within him loosened, everything physical and spiritual, then it all went away as he smashed onto the ground. *Such little pain* he thought, *so little pain.*

And they had him again, dragging him, cursing and kicking because he had soiled himself. Back into the barracks. The helicopter, which had never been higher than ten feet made a shy bow, then rode its growling engine into the night.

Jimmy lay in the dim light of this new room, it was warm, and there was a wooden floor and then the hands again.

Now the soft embrace of these hands was all that mattered to the man under the hood. The hands were life, legitimacy, power. They were clean, they were everything Jimmy was not, and he wanted them, wanted more than anything to have their approval. And in the warm room with the wooden floor and gentle light, Jimmy broke. In this place he was without time, where the borders of his flesh no longer separated him from anything, so that his name, his existence, no longer mattered, he broke and he only wanted to be again, to obtain the love of the strong man with the loving hands.

His life that had been, drifted away, and his new life passed from the hands to his new being, and they had him.

At that moment he felt the most pure love for his tormentors and he kissed the hands and thought, *truly this is the love of which Jesus spoke.* Jimmy had never felt such love, and hooded on the floor of the barracks Jimmy wept and smiled through bloody lips. And as he lay there, time, peace, and his name slowly flowed back and filled him.

The hands massaged his temples as he talked, they pressed a clean handkerchief to his eyes and mouth and nose and he kept talking. Names, addresses, hiding places for weapons in homes, near trees and on steep riverbanks.

He talked and never had he known such happiness, such trust, such pure relief.

More men came and carried him to the toilet and let him take a shower, then back to the room with the wooden floor and the embrace of the policeman who gave him a cigarette, hugged him and said,

"I know, Jimmy, I know."

Chief Detective Ian MacDonald gently tugged the right knee of his trousers as he crouched down. The suit was dark brown with subtle strips of very dark blue. At age 37 MacDonald was a thick-set man who could be very patient and gruff in turn.

He was moody, with a dry wit mixing with a temper that could snap to the fore in an instant. He had begun his career in law enforcement at age 22 as a uniformed member of the Royal Ulster Constabulary. The RUC. He didn't make waves, he was meticulous, had street smarts, was neither popular nor shunned by colleagues. Ian MacDonald did well on tests both written and physical. Ian MacDonald advanced to sergeant, then out of uniform to detective in the RUC's Special Branch. The elite of Northern Ireland, the feared, the respected.

He was fascinated by seeds and the plants that came forth from them. He had a lovely garden, a pleasant wife and a little boy, Nigel, seven years old, whom he adored and who in turn adored him.

Bad news could set Detective MacDonald to a foul mood for days. But on the floor before him was good news, very good news indeed. That news lay in the form of the bleeding broken man on these wide wooden boards.

Here was a piece of one of the most feared terrorist groups in the world. Upon these few wide planks was legend and song, poem and history. The car bomb, the kidnapper, judge and jury, masked executioner, an L-shaped ambush cutting down British soldiers like a spoiled child swiping at his toys. Here was the Irish Republican Army.

The IRA. Too-white skinned, bruised yellow and blue, whimpering, blood still dripping here and there, testicles still swollen from English boots, stained underwear, dirty hair with fine lumps beneath, now in the fetal position. Here was Jimmy Fitzgerald floating on a pond of Catholic shame. Here was opportunity, as if like a loving sculptor, Detective MacDonald could summon forth all that lay beneath.

"Jimmy, I'm going to send you home now." He saw the nod of the bruised head. "Jimmy, this is our secret. Me and you. We're in this together. Just the two of us."

Detective MacDonald smothered his rage and loathing and reached out to press the fingers of one hand to the prisoner's head.

The RUC met with other law enforcement agencies from around the world. They exchanged information, insights in the shadowy groups they fought. Detective MacDonald didn't mind telling others about the IRA's methods and means.

But he kept to himself what made them uniquely Irish. How a race of singers and poets, drinkers and jokers could cross a line. A boundary that ran behind those lovely blue eyes, dwelling where there was absolutely no forgiveness, no sympathy. It was latent within this people. If they felt wronged, insulted, pushed, it would come forth and it would never go away. Then came forth racial memory, tribal rage, a people without mercy.

"Just the two of us lad. No one else knows. Neither your comrades nor mine." The detective smoothed the hair, could feel a lump and pressed it ever so softly.

"Our lives are bound together now lad, they're interwoven. Think of the colors of a sunrise, one doesn't end before the other begins. We're like that Jimmy. You and I lad, we are those colors."

The detective let the words sink in, then said,

"You're to be released now. Just be yourself. Move forward. Do nothing differently and you will hear from me, understand?"

"I do."

"What's the phone number?"

Jimmy told him the phone number he was to call every five days at noon.

"Good, Jimmy, it's good you understand. Remember, I will know, and I will contact you at the appropriate time."

The detective stood, brushed off his hands and left the soundproof room. The man on the floor rolled over and pulled himself to a sitting position, knees up, arms on knees, head upon the arms. He didn't look up until the soldiers came and yanked him to his feet. Sergeant Albert Roberts, 34, of the Royal Anglians, stood at ease and listened to his instructions. Intense, ruddy, short, powerful, with premature grey flecks in his closely trimmed moustache that had earned him the nickname Sergeant Pepper.

The directions came from a detective, while Sergeant Robert's commanding officer stood silently to one side. That alone told the sergeant all he needed to know. Once again the civilians were meddling in military matters, and as usual making a muck of the show. He'd seen it in Aden, he'd seen it on Cyprus. Now he was seeing it in Northern Ireland.

The civilians got in over their heads and screamed for the army to rescue them. Then, just when the army had the enemy by the throat the bloody civilians would come out from under the bed and take over again.

Be civilized they'd say, play nice. Don't want the Yanks upset, don't want the Russians angry, don't want the bloody Eskimos with their furry knickers in a knot.

When the copper had finished his blather about rights and limits on interrogation and new rules from Whitehall, Captain Cross spoke up.

"Well, that's the nutshell then. We know the bloke's IRA but there's no more we can do. He held out for the seven day limit, now he's to be released. Of course we'll keep a close eye on him. And your delivering him home, as it were, sends a message. Shows we're on top of things. Gets the wind up the bogtrotters' sails. Sets a standard as it were."

"A standard, Sir."

"Quite right sergeant."

"Yes, Sir."

"Good, sergeant. Glad you see this clearly. Carry on."

"Yes, Sir."

As he walked back to his squad, Sergeant Roberts muttered to himself. *I'd deliver the bastard home alright. In a fucking pine box. Or with two bullets in the back of his empty fucking head and throw 'im through his front fucking door.* By the time he reached his men, lounging about their armored car, he was nearly apoplectic.

"Stand 'round!" he shouted at his soldiers. "We're now a terrorist fucking taxi service. We're to take Paddy pig-fucker back home so he can rest up a while before trying to kill us. Any questions?"

Two squaddies started to speak but the sergeant roiled over them, screaming, "Well I don't want to hear them! Now get that piece of shit and put 'im in the Saracen!"

Above the man on the floor of the armored car, in two rows of three, the young faces were English, their lips thick and moist, cheeks that blushed with exertion or excitement, dignity always intact. Dignity that could morph instantly to contempt.

Jimmy avoided their eyes as the armored car bumped and twisted its way through Belfast.

"Paddy."

Jimmy looked up at the sergeant who had spoken.

"We know who you are. We know where you are. We know what you are."

Jimmy kept his eyes closed.

"Paddy, look at me!"

Jimmy did, feeling their packgaze on him as their leader spoke.

"If you are anywhere nearby my squad when so much as a fucking balloon pops I will personally kill you. I will shoot you and piss on you as you die. Got that, you filthy fucking Irish pig?"

"I understand."

The sergeant's threat was all the more menacing because it was whispered.

"Make sure you do Paddy, make sure you do."

The vehicle kept bouncing, which saved him from some of the blows. Then a rock clanged off the side, then another and another. Jimmy heard a soldier mutter,

"Fucking kids."

Inside their metal cocoon fear nipped at their feet, snapped at them with the hollow thudding of every bottle and rock bouncing off the Saracen.

The British Army had put its boots on these streets four years earlier. They'd done so to stop Protestant mobs from burning down these Catholic homes, to replace the Protestant police reserves, the B-specials, who had gone mad with rage, bigotry and automatic weapons.

Singing "We Shall Overcome," the Catholics had at long last made a grab for civil rights, for jobs, for one man one vote. And the state had almost crushed them. Almost.

The leaders of Protestant Ulster brought down every weapon they could raise to hammer them back into their priest-infested Roman Catholic hovels, as they had done so many times in the last four centuries.

But they would not go. Not this time. Shot, beaten, gassed, they would not break. And with anarchy loose, the world watching in disbelief, the British Army arrived.

They tried. But they were the cops summoned to break up an unending domestic dispute. They just wanted everyone to calm down and go back to the way things were. But calm had long abandoned the Protestant majority, and the Catholic minority was not going anywhere, least of all back.

The great green machine of the British military quickly found itself becoming Yeats's rude beast, its Irish time at last come 'round again, slouching toward morass, where all sin was original, all forgiveness excommunicated. From gentlemen officers to semiliterate boys from the grime of East London, all the soldiers understood this. Intellectually or emotionally, at some level, they knew. And they only wanted to get through this day, this tour, to survive these hordes of freckle-faced Zulus and go home.

Now the houses were closer to the street, the people too were closer, seeming ready to reach inside the Saracen to kill. The kids were throwing everything they could lift as the armored car went further into the ghetto. Block after block went past, each of the buildings seeming to conjure up its own small mob, bursting onto the sidewalks, all focused on the Saracen.

The men in camouflage stopped kicking and grew tense as they went deeper into this hostile neighborhood. The driver shouted "Hey!" and threw up his hands as a thick milk bottle banged the view slit in front of him, showering shards of glass on his lap and across the metal floor.

Getting up, the sergeant crouched with one arm on the driver's shoulder as they both peered ahead. They saw one-story brick houses flow past, houses with broken windows, broken roof tiles, some with broken walls. They saw swarms of kids in short pants, racing for rocks and bottles to hurl at them, saw older boys in jeans glaring, observed men and women studiously ignoring the rumbling armored vehicle.

They felt, could almost see, waves of hostility directed at them, as the huge armored car rumbled along, shaking window panes, waking babies, causing women to press hands to their throats and to stir within men the special rage of the weak.

Turning, the sergeant motioned to the two soldiers at the back, who grabbed the rear doors handles. Then he took hold of Jimmy, as the armored car changed gears and tried to run down some young stone throwers. As the vehicle accelerated the sergeant spoke.

"This is your stop, Paddy."

Standing in her doorway, 70-year-old Mary Burke thought the soldiers had flung a bag of trash at her. She screamed when she realized it was a broken man, his skin a rainbow of brutality, his only garment a pair of undershorts, his pathetic attempts to stand increasing her fright, causing her to scream louder.

Women came running, children cascaded upon the scene as men pushed to the front to see. Arms held the battered man. Women's hands brushed the hair from his face as they carried him inside the Burke's home. He was washed, towels were pressed around him, clothes the right size were found, warm whiskey was pressed to his lips.

He was moved, and moved again. Men carried him over back fences and through houses from one back street to the next and then the one beyond.

Other men came, men who caused those present to step back. No one greeted these men by name. Some nodded to them, some pretended not to see them. These were silent men with the chill of October nights in their gaze. They were not big men, not muscular, not loud, but men with a leanness, a steady presence, men with a weight to their stance. Mature men who could control themselves, men who could hold the rage the sight of Jimmy set off within them. Men who used the heat of that rage only at certain times, and only under very certain circumstances. It was these men who bore Jimmy away.

They took him to silence. In a second floor room they let him sleep on a cot. They gave him food and drink and they put him in a chair facing an empty wall, and the silence held him immobile.

Behind Jimmy footfalls drew near and drifted off, voices, one or two he recognized, spoke in whispers. The wall was dim yellow, with bits of white plaster peeking out where the years had curled the yellow back. Jimmy pictured someone painting this wall long ago, and he waited.

It may have been two or even six hours later when he heard them coming. Slow steps, soft footfalls, coming up the stairs, two, maybe three of them. Then they were close behind. He could hear the movements as they removed hats and coats. And there was something else. There was a wafting fragrance of fields from these men. Fields and the fertile scents of animals, he imagined their hair short and all awry in the way of rural people.

In the silence they let their presence pin him to the yellow wall. Let all his transgressions scream inside his skull, and they did nothing.

"*God, speak,*" he thought. "*Say something.*"

But they did not, and the day dimmed.

Finally one, and only one, spoke. He probed like a doctor poking for a foreign object in a patient. Very carefully he inquired, and Jimmy answered to the blank wall. The unseen man went over all the questions, sometimes asking them from a different direction, but always drawing the thread back to center. Always working on the knot. Jimmy saw his late mother with dress and apron, sewing, sewing, then with a quick move she would break the thread, biting off the end. He shivered.

They left and let him sleep. They woke him in darkness, and the questions circled him and he dropped his answers, and they too circled his throat. They let him sleep again and woke him. Still it was dark.

Such patient men. So thorough thought Jimmy. Farm men used to time without watches or radios, time governed by seasons and sun. *God forgive me*, thought Jimmy as he lied to them, and the lies fell into the water with everything else that swam round and round him. And they let him sleep.

He woke to daylight growing fuller, heard very soft voices on the stairs, women's voices. A woman, middle aged, grey haired, came in with a tray of food and she smiled at him. He had not seen a human smile since the police had taken away time. Now time was back, and he could only nod and take in the warmth of this woman. She left without a word and he knew he was, as much as he would ever in his life be again, safe.

He stayed in that place for three days and nights. His injuries receded, his strength returned, the face in the mirror began to reclaim what had been its own.

The grey haired woman came twice a day and she fussed over him, praising his courage and his sacrifice. She told him just her first name and never asked for his. She had raised sons and daughters in this impoverished place, had strengthened her man and stood up for what was right. She was Irish, Catholic, God-fearing, witty, smart, and well-read. This ghetto was full of women just like her. They were tougher than the men, smarter, healthier, more realistic. And perhaps their greatest strength was pretending along with everyone else that it was not so.

"I think I'll go for a walk," he told her.

"If you're up to it, luv."

"I'm sure I am."

He took the stairs with fingers spread against the wall for reassurance. Then he stepped out onto the street, inhaling peat smoke, taking in the air and sky above. He crossed the street with the setting sun, nodding to the ones who recognized him, almost smiling once, walking down Leeson Street with its gentle incline. He turned left and right without purpose, touching the heads of little children, drawing strength from them, almost feeling hope. Inside he felt a black wet cloth arranged across his soul. It clung, it pressed his lungs, it marked him in God's eye for the coward and traitor he had become. And he walked as the sun fled and the moon hove over Belfast Lough's horizon.

Retracing his steps, walking quicker now, feeling the chill of a Belfast night and all the horrors it let loose, he had to will himself not to run into the pub. When he entered there was an audible pause in conversation, broken by his friend Louis Duffy who, arms spread wide proclaimed,

"And on the third day he rose from the fucken' dead and decided to have a pint."

Louis Duffy, 29, childhood friend become surrogate big brother, five foot nine, brown eyes, light brown hair loose and free as the spirit within the man. Husband, father, joker, dart player, pool shooter, football fan, gentle, sensitive, kind. Louis Duffy nourished a lifelong goal of hearing a jazz band play in New Orleans. He was also a skilled carpenter, passable electrician, part time auto mechanic, full time IRA guerrilla.

Louis draped an arm around Jimmy, guiding him to the bar, as he announced,

"He is risen, halleluiah. He is no longer of flesh and blood but dwells in the spirit. Get this fucken' spirit a drink."

Louis guided his friend to the end of the bar, keeping a hand on his shoulder, steadying the freed prisoner, standing close, a firm buffer against whatever the room might present. With the pint glasses dripping before them, Louis squeezed his friend's shoulder to whisper,

"Ya alright then?"

Jimmy glanced at the other man, then looked at the beer.

"Alright, I guess. Felt like they had me for seven years instead of seven days."

Louis, glancing at their reflections in the mirror behind the bar, nodded.

"Aye. Same for meself. Don't they love their work, though?"

Louis still had his personal nightmare from interrogation. He had been tied down on a table while a man gently drummed his fingers on his abdomen. Such a small indignity at first. Almost silly. Until the walls of the stomach begin to crumble and the victim feels he is impaled on a hot sword. Then the gentle fingers turn into the instrument of a sadistic maestro. Louis, watching their reflections in the glass, unconsciously cupping a hand to his stomach, asked himself one more time, *Who thinks up such things to do to another man?*

After a gulp of the beer, Jimmy spoke.

"They wouldn't let me sleep. Three days, four days, five days, I don't know. I was seeing things, seeing people who weren't there. Hearin' them. Dead people, live people. They was all there. Some just talkin', some just lookin', some screamin' at me. Imagine, just bein' awake can do that to ya. I hollered back. Didn't know if I was yellin' at the ghosts or the fucken Special Branch."

Louis looked askance at his companion.

"I know," was all he said. Louis didn't mention what they had done to his stomach. It was too embarrassing, to be held down and touched by other men like that. It was shameful, and except for the IRA debriefers, he had never told anyone about it.

As the pair drank, a few men ambled by to wish Jimmy well. An older woman came to kiss him on the cheek and recall him as a wee boy full of mischief and laughter. Always Louis stood close, his stance subtly telling them to keep it brief, to greet without questioning. They all did, and again Jimmy and Louis were alone.

They talked a bit about sports, about Louis's three children, about a rent strike at the nearby housing complex, Divis Flats. Then, with the path ahead pocked with open wounds, they fell into silence until Jimmy said he was pretty tired and thought he'd turn in for the night. Louis said,

"Some of the lads want a pint with ye' tomorrow night. Be some ladies there as well. Up for it?"

"I am."

Louis smiled.

"Good, get some rest then. An' we'll see ya tomorrow right here."

At the doorway they nodded to the five teenage boys clustered there. Unarmed, the boys stood to sound the alarm at the approach of soldiers, to watch the neighborhood, to assist the IRA in any way they could. Every pub and social club in the area had such boys. And there were hundreds of pubs and social clubs in the district. The boys were part of a thin membrane that lay across the ghetto, a nervous system that registered every stranger's approach, every unusual occurrence, every wish of the IRA.

The boys peered out in every direction, monitoring the smoky gloom. Here the IRA had shot out every streetlight and the British army had painted walls black to hide their counter-ambush teams. Here was pure night, fog and fear, a place where Jack the Ripper could be expected in any doorway. Jack was long gone, but his heirs were about the streets, zipping by in cars without headlights, guns out windows. The Butcher Gang was on the prowl looking for Catholics to slowly slaughter, limb by limb, organ by organ. No one wanted to stray too far in Belfast these damp and cozy nights, none but the sons of Jack.

Michaela Murphy negotiated the blackness, monitoring its ebony clues, noting the familiar inky blur of neighborhood buildings. Moving off the incline of Leeson Street she turned into the lane where her rooms awaited. So many feared this dark, these broken streetlights waiting forever for someone to mend their jagged wounds, the walls of century-old buildings bleeding moisture into clinging fog. But Michaela did not allow any of that to enter, to dwell within with its doubts and fear-filled future. She rejected that chaos, that robbing of the heart.

Michaela breathed deeply, exhaling as slowly as she could, letting the dark brush her fingertips making her approaching pleasure even more sensual. Michaela Murphy, 24, brown eyed, five foot five, single, brunette, beauty, and daughter of this place, was dying for a cigarette. She would hold her unlit cigarette as she walked among her three rooms. Then she would extinguish the lights, settle in her chair, and meld with the cigarette, letting it become an understanding friend. A friend with memories in its twisting smoke, gossip in the retreat of its glowing tip, acceptance in each drawn breath. And when the cigarette had given its grace, Michaela prayed; not with words but with what this silent room said to her.

That this life of hers was meant to be, that her mother taken by death from five-year-old Michaela, her da gone soon after, was part of what made Michaela the woman she was. That from pain came strength and yes, also beauty. She could see beauty within others. And she could see the festering wounds of those who thought only of themselves. Those who reveled in jealousy, pettiness, who sipped delightedly from others' painful falls, the ones who ran bellowing with the stampeding herd. Jesus had seen them too. They stood at the front of the temple, posing not praying, and calling out not for God but for attention. Pharisees. Oh, they were still about, maybe they were the same souls tumbling through time, never learning, never satisfied, never understanding there was not enough gold in the world to buy them contentment. They were still around all right. On the telly, in the newspaper, at the pubs, full of bluster, full of their grasping needs, full of themselves.

The cigarette ran down, finished off with rapid taps on a saucer as Michaela stepped out of her clothes to wash at the sink. She stood upon a deep rug not much wider than she was, while nearby a folded towel waited, crowding a face cloth, shampoo and soap.

Michaela moved slowly, simultaneously washing away the day while letting it become part of her. Drying very carefully she slipped into a white robe and two slippers, flattened at the heels, as she mused, *so familiar, so formed to my feet, how could I ever part with them?*

Before bed, she brushed her teeth, and in front of the mirror dabbed cream, seeing what she loved and what she wished she could change. Minutes later Michaela lay still on the bed, both hands clasped behind her head, eyes open, feeling the dark and everything in it move past her, around her, through her.

She could see her life with the man she would love. Could feel the press of her fingertips to his cheek, could hear the timbre of his voice, not his words, but his voice, she could imagine his scent, his smile, his eyes. These aspects of the man came into focus and out again. She could feel his touch, the curve of his hands and arms but not hold his face in focus. He stood before her mind in silhouette, a sliver of pale light here, a glint there, and then he stepped back into the surrounding mists.

Would he step away forever? Will I be a woman alone, the aunt, the cousin, the friend, single and happy? Envied and the envy turning to pity with the passing years? *No man, poor woman, alone in that house, and so attractive more's the pity. Girl alone, young woman by herself, unescorted lady, poor, poor, poor old thing.*

No not me. If I grow old alone so be it. I'll wear my wrinkles and make people laugh and maybe cry with the stories of people met and foreign places seen. I must see Rome and all the ancient Greek temples, dried white as white can be from 3,000 years of wanting the sun.

Didn't it all start with the Greeks and Romans? All civilization passed down? But not ours. Not our druids and pagan rites. Oh, and the Vikings too, they came here to this island. They feared neither waters nor any man. All in my blood, my life, mine alone.

With thoughts of longboats, taut sails red and white, swiftly closing on green shores, Michaela Murphy slipped into sleep.

Stepping onto the morning sidewalk Michaela felt the comfort of this day's outfit, felt the swirl of her dress, the tips of her raven hair touching her forehead with each step forward. She smiled and that smile touched the people she passed. The grumpiest of the old men, children flowing past at a run, the middle-aged women with their forever limps and myriad burdens, they all caught that smile and returned it.

Michaela felt the Lower Falls coming awake, stretching, shifting its weight, ready to take stock of what had passed in the night. She let the breeze take all of that, for this was her day, her time, her life and soul. She understood that, and she knew, all within her was a key, and when the moment was right that key would unlock so many many things.

As Jimmy strode along, his mind drifted back to a time when he was simply the youngest of three, the one who could never catch up to the two brothers ahead as they broke new trails. It was left for him to tread the echo of their exuberance, to wish the parental audience to thrill at this repeat performance. Belfast boyhood had held him tight in its camaraderie, in the pride of the outcasts, in their world of the alley and rooftop.

Then when Jimmy was 16, flu moved through the city, coughs became groans and the groans became the death of his beloved middle brother Thomas. Jimmy, weak from the disease himself, staggered through a wake, a funeral mass, a graveside service where the November sun blinded and chilled them all in its search for what had been.

And then home. To Ma taken to a chair in a dim corner, Da to his spot at the bar, an oldest brother soon off to England.

Briefly Jimmy sought solace in the cathedral, in its stainglassed montage, its leaping ceiling, the incense and bereft organ pipes. He called, he pleaded, fasted and offered up for the souls in purgatory. He told God he didn't need a miracle, only the smallest of signs on these moral steppes. The answer was the vast expanse of the building, echoing coughs of parishioners, a collection plate hurried along like earth's own orphan.

In a year Da was gone, in two Ma was turned into a thrashing presence on sweat soaked sheets, and again all went to the graveside, again the too little words sprinkled over her.

In a few days he held a meeting with his big brother to divide nothing into two. Then brother went back to England and Jimmy returned to street corner and wall.

He became a young man respected at cards and darts, snooker, billiards and divining winning steeds. He found occasional work in bricklaying, lorry driving, and when things were lean, at the slaughterhouses. And when things got even leaner he stood staring at scuffed shoes before the dole.

In times good and bad, always he wanted more, wanted to touch what he saw on the telly. California beaches, redwoods brushing clouds, Mississippi girls wearing white dresses, tossing powder and lace to ward off men's lust. He wanted to hear a southern sheriff, pot bellied and mean, his swagger kicking up dust, tell his quarry,

"You in trouble now, boy."

He held his daydreams tight, learning to ration them, to press their warm rainbows to his chest and to wait for his moment, which he was sure would soon come.

He puzzled at the indignation and words of the Catholic civil rights marchers striding across Northern Ireland. He felt shared pride at how they pushed and bent the oppressive rules, saw the coppers lash out. He could only shake his head at the nonviolent boys and girls who got off the ground and stood right back up to the coppers. It made something stir in him, in all of them. They could see it. The law saw it too, and the law went mad.

Over a week into it he strolled from a doorway, two Molotov cocktails in his hands, and stood waiting for the coppers. And they came, and saw him alone, and the group of them stopped. Because they were afraid.

That moment, when he saw them step backward because he alone confronted them, that potent mix of anger, fear and eroticism propelled him into the secret army. And that oath, that great change allowed him to understand that huge change is easier than the small daily adjustments, the unending compromise of the normal. Easier because you have a new identity, the people who never really saw you now act with respect. Rumors precede you and they can ease the way.

And he came to know something else. You're still you. Wearing your new cloak is no different than a child digging a hole in beach sand. One way or the other, eventually the truth will flow into it.

Then you'll be what you've always been. Another bloke kidding himself, pressed tight to life's little round table, wanting to stay, wanting to leave, waiting for the cards to be dealt.

Louis Duffy, eight, stood beside his father in the rain, man and boy in front of the dwelling like penitents before a shrine. The January wind nipped at them, snapping their clothing, pushing the rain sideways, pulling heat from their faces, necks, and hands.

The father and son each held a short shovel with a wide blade. They waited, and waited.

Louis's father, so quick-tempered at home, now stood still, letting the downpour permeate his clothing and flesh. The man's head was bowed, and his son took his cue from that and looked at the rivulets forming around his own feet.

Finally the woman who had answered their knock reappeared at the window and jerked a thumb toward the back of the house. They followed her instruction and again stood before a door, this one smaller and made of faded brown wood, leading to a basement.

"Da, I'm soaked through completely."

"Quiet."

Louis heard the inside latch snap, but the door did not open and he and his father remained motionless as the rain continued to embrace them. Then a woman's voice, sounding far away told them,

"It's open."

The father pulled the door wide and descended into the gloom, his son close behind. The irritated woman had retreated to the lighted world above them.

"Touch nothin' but what you're hired to touch. We keep a

strict inventory."

Gentle curses played on his father's lips as Louis felt his face flush.

"She thinks we're thieves," he told himself. "She thinks me an' my da are thieves."

Louis's eyes met those of his father, and the angry man's face softened and he reached out to cup his son's head in a wide calloused palm.

"Don't be makin' off with her coal," he whispered, adding, "Don't be stealin' none a' the cobwebs down here."

They were to remove the coal from the wooden bin, carry it outside and place it on a tarp. They were to sweep the coal bin clean and dispose of the sweepings. This home was being converted to central heating. It was to run on gas. The woman had mentioned that to Louis's father numerous times. The message was repeated to reinforce another message left unsaid. *We are Protestant. You are Catholic. We have central heating. You burn turf in tiny stoves. You are inferior. But we are fair. We pay you. Now do as you are told.*

All that morning they gently slid shovels beneath tumbling coal, lifting ever so gently, trying unsuccessfully to not cause black dust. They walked gingerly into the rain to deposit their treasure, then back into the gloom. When done they swept the bin clean, the coal dust now finding them, clinging, highlighting sweat, anger and pride. Making bluer their eyes, whiter the skin around them, such white circles drawn by the black coal. And they were done.

Again they were made to stand in the downpour and wait. The water streaking their faces and hands, his father nudging him.

"Here's an Irishman's fancy bath."

They both chuckled, and finally the woman, apparently having carefully counted everything in the cellar, handed the money over. She might as well have thrown the coins at them.

Afterwards, the laughter of the men at the round table lifted the boy, his father's strong arm holding him tight as Louis rode their currents of joy his da declaring,

"Bloody inventory of the cellar. Thought she'd look up me arse to see if I'd some of her precious coal stuck up there."

Another wave of laughter buoyed Louis, lifted him like a gentle warm wave, and his father rubbed his head. At this table father and son wore their black dust like badges of honor, as the boy saw his world click into place like a delicate mechanism. He understood now that those others looked down on him, his family, these fine men around him. He understood and accepted and became stronger.

That afternoon at that round table with his father, their wool and flannel clothing slowly drying amid the smell of beer, amid the whispered thuds of darts against a nearby board, Louis and his father sealed an unspoken bond.

Both understood the lesson. *I am your father but they treat me like a child. I am a man and they will not acknowledge my manhood. See this, understand it, stand up to it when you can. This is our country. Often we can only fight them with our humor. Resist.*

He grew ever closer to his father as he took on the role of eldest child. He was responsible, hardworking, the protector of the younger ones. He could use his fists if he had to, and at times everyone here had to.

In his last teenage year his father sat across from him gathering ashtray, matches and cigarettes and began to tell a story. Then he stopped and slumped back so easily Louis thought it was part of the tale. And just like that his da was gone.

When all the words were said, all the hands shaken, all the hugs come and gone, Louis stepped onto the streets as the man of the house, his mother's rock, his siblings' protector. He did not stagger beneath this new load. Rather he accepted it, as he accepted where he lived, when he lived, and the invisible forces that held all of it in place. He never thought of himself as being disadvantaged. Treated unfairly, yes, but that was life. They were all treated unfairly, and had been for centuries. Louis Duffy was not one to complain. He was one to deal with reality.

He married a woman he loved and who loved him. She gave birth and he loved her even more. His life was settled, he was a contented man when the Catholic students began their civil rights marches.

Louis thought them naïve at best, perhaps troublemakers in a place where there was always a surplus of trouble. Then the youngsters marching for civil rights were attacked by the police. They were not told to disperse, they were pummeled. Arrested, they were not charged. They were bludgeoned. The nonviolence of educated youth was met with the brute force of aroused power. Reason was introduced to rage.

Then things didn't so much erupt as the ground opened and they all fell into a black maw. The only light was the flames of rioting, the only sound the innocent screaming, the only thought was of winning. And in the ghetto, the sudden burning understanding that this time they were not going to beat us to the pavement. This time we, all of us, were going to fight or die.

Louis found his easy camaraderie with men translated into an ability to lead. Men would listen to him, they would follow because he was always by their side or in front of them.

If his child's birth had created in Louis something new, now the explosion of human emotion brought forth another dimension of this Falls Road man.

He never wavered, never felt fear, and knew only the burning light of a single goal. To make the State admit that he and his comrades were men. The State refused. And Louis and the small circle that acknowledged him as leader would not yield.

Hundreds of men like Louis came to the fore and thousands followed them. They knew very few things for certain. But they all understood that now there would be no turning back.

Very quickly rocks and Molotov cocktails were exchanged for rifles and explosives. Louis moved steadily through every transition.

When arrested he was threatened, then beaten, then tortured. Louis Duffy never wavered, never talked, never looked back, never hated.

When released he took up where he'd left off. Leading by example, planning with precision, killing without rancor.

Always he loved his family, his religion, his nation that would one day be. He didn't count the days, the cost, or the maimed and the dead.

He had a gift of fine athletes. He saw the whole picture, he saw what was about to happen a split second before anyone else. He knew when to attack, when to retreat and when to stay still.

In a neighborhood wired tight with crackling emotion, instant news, spontaneous rumor, in a place where a man was known by the street he was born on, Louis's reputation grew. His accolades were all earned, and the highest of them was his moniker "our Louis."

Beyond any field manual or tome on guerrilla warfare, beyond tactics and theory, Louis survived and thrived for a very simple reason. The people loved him.

Louis didn't dwell on any of it. God had put him on earth for a reason, put him in a particular time to face His infinite challenges. Louis left the big ideas to the ones with the big minds. He was a simple man and he saw this as a simple thing. He would never stand with his son and be talked down to by some Loyalist housewife all full of herself and the Union Jack. Not him. Not his boy. Really, it was that clear. He could see it, and someday the lords and ladies would see it too.

The match Louis held to light Jimmy's cigarette flared a blinding yellow, emitting a sulfurous snarl, and like so many things now, it startled Jimmy. Louis lit his own cigarette with the same match then spoke, the cigarette on his lips bouncing to his words.

"I met murder along the way. He had a face like Castlereagh."

Louis squinted at his comrade-in-arms, who stood with his back pressed to a brick wall, a man who had just fled his own welcome-home party.

"Jimmy, us ones that been there understand. We know. It's fine to be on the jittery side. It's normal. We know the feelings ya got. When you're ready to come back to the unit tell me and I'll tell the others."

Louis looked at the man whose gaze was upon the wet pavement, and softly told Jimmy what he himself had endured at Castleraegh. Stripped naked and made to run a gauntlet of soldiers with batons, made to lean against a wall for hours while being punched and kicked, grabbed by the hair, his head repeatedly banged against a wall. Sleep deprivation, a screaming man, blood all down his front leaping from another room waving a bayonet, slaps to the ears, the loss of time, of dignity, almost the loss of self.

"But no ride in a helicopter. Guess I'm not worth the cost of the petrol."

Jimmy looked up saying, "Some ride."

Louis took Jimmy by the shoulders.

"Aye, some ride. Some ride we're all on."

His head tilted down, Jimmy thought, *He is pure and I am not. He will see through me and know, and he'll cry when they have to kill me.*

Finishing his cigarette and without another word Louis took Jimmy by the arm, leading the way back inside to announce,

"Make way, the Red Baron's in for a landing."

They embraced Jimmy, the women with hugs and tearful pecks to his cheeks, the men with handshakes and pats on the back. Louis shouted,

"Free helicopter tours of Belfast! God, don't the English love the Irish!"

The laughter came over Jimmy like a warm breeze and he thought, *I love you all, I'll tell them nothing, I'll trick the Brits like they tricked me, I'll protect you all. For Ireland, for Ireland.* He took the pint glass they pressed upon him and said aloud,

"For Ireland."

All present repeated his words and a fiddle sounded from a corner and a tin whistle joined in. The men came forward, taking women by elbows and hands, guiding them with arms around their thin waists, and the women embraced the dance.

Outside a soft rain was falling on narrow streets, broken buildings and perfect darkness. The Catholic ghetto of the Falls Road hugged the ground tight as British soldiers and the IRA silently maneuvered, awaiting the chance to kill one another. Maybe the night riders would come, speeding out of Protestant Shankill to gun down Catholic pedestrians. Perhaps a car bomb would *whumph* its instantaneous birth and death.

Tight black fists of fear were in all of them at some level all the time. But those fears only raised the curtain to the terror that rode with the Butcher Gang. The ones who came in cars on these nights to snatch Catholics off the curb and butcher them alive. Meat hooks and piano wire, castration and worse, skin off by the layer, things you can't imagine, they told one another. And they imagined. Out of the night and no one saw, no one heard, until a boy did not come home, a couple was not seen, a man did not stop in for his pint.

Run, they told one another, *run. They'll shoot you in the back if you run. But if they get you, oh lad if they get you, then when they finally put the gun to your head, you'll say 'Thank You.'*

All this was in the damp atmosphere of the Falls, and in Jimmy too as he watched the dancers, having begged off taking the floor due to lingering pain. But the pain was gone now, turned and twisted away, a cloud dissolving among other clouds. It had moved across his sky, it had drifted from him. Like everything and everyone, it was at a distance. And Jimmy watched the dancers and he waited and he tensed and relaxed, then grew rigid again.

Wait, he had been instructed. *Just wait. Do nothing different and we will contact you. Just be yourself.* Now he did what had deserted him at Castleraegh. He saw the perfect candle, could almost hear the breath of its yellow flame, saw it bend left, straighten, bend right. Lifting his hands he could sense its burning gift to the cold night. The candle was so clear its flame whispered to him, it whispered and was gone. Jimmy blinked and heard the policeman's instruction.

Be yourself. Just move on.

Jimmy stood, wanting to join the dance, wanting the freedom of movement. But he could only be still while feeling all that moved within.

Michaela Murphy had the dream again, this dream of her mother, who had died young. As always the dream had held tiny pennants of color in attendance of her mother, the flash of her red sweater, the silky sliding of her white slip as she dressed and powdered. Michaela thought, *did I run my palm over its gentle surface?* Her mother letting her blue dress fall over her shoulders, lovely shoulders, lovely woman, a silver crucifix at her neck.

Her mother young and laughing. Michaela could see her laughing, the wonderful curve of her full lips, her teeth so fine. In the dream Michaela could see all of it, but could not hear a sound. Her mother smiling, gesturing, speaking to the little girl, but the words did not reach the child. *Mummy.*

Michaela Murphy came awake to her three rooms, her ceiling, her window with its bright yellow curtain. She stretched, then in one movement she flipped back the covers and hopped off the bed. At the sink she contemplated the girl in the mirror as she thought, *I'm almost her age. That short a life, that brief a time, that long in dreams.*

Appearing taller than her five-foot-four height, raven hair cut short, eyes two brown pools that held and warned, a smile to embrace life, a face with the flashing moods of an early spring sky. She stepped outside into wounds carried by the breeze. She saw the knot of men at the corner, staring at the newly opened innards of a vacant building. Its side had been torn down two nights ago by a British armored car.

People said the driver was drunk, or he hit the building deliberately to send the neighborhood a message, others insisted he'd panicked at some sound and careened into the empty house.

Whatever the cause the area had a new landmark, a new focal point, some spanking new debris to go with all the old. Michaela thought, *Some day we will build and not knock down. I'll see that day. They'll cut ribbons in the sunshine for a new library, a school, a store full of pretty clothes and fragrances. I'll see that day. I'm young, I'll watch that sliced ribbon float free, I'll hold a child's hand in that store amid the blossoming of a hundred perfumes.*

Beyond that crisp canvas, past the edge of what she could bring into focus, was the presence of a man. A man who would hold her hand as they walked, who would press her tight and speak of his love for her.

Boys had gone from being cute to groping oafs, they were awkward children and cold blooded conquerors. Once she felt she was almost in love, and once she was sure she would never know love. Then young men came like gathering waves, great and green as they reared up in towering strength, promising this time would be different. Then they were gone to white mist and memory, leaving only emotion's smooth retreating pebbles as the ocean drew another breath.

That was her and boys, that was her and young men, until The Troubles grabbed everyone by the collar and yanked them into the streets.

Michaela never threw a rock or a curse. Rather she tended the injured in a steady stream, guided by a nurse who was guided over a phone by a doctor. Walking down a row of male bodies, learning to respond quickly to the harsh commands: *Bandage, splint, roll him over, lift him up. Leave him, leave him luv, he's gone.*

Everyone sleeping in shifts to hold off the Loyalist mobs, the battle suddenly shifting as the swarms pushed closer. The tribal screams, a million voices out of the darkness, cacophonous and two-noted, the primal become vocal. *God help us.* Every hair on her body bristling, *Jesus in heaven help us.* Her arms and scalp chilled, the screams fading again in the night's blackness. *Holy Mary, mother of God, now and at the hour.*

Their little clinic moving back as the berserk enemy lunged, moving the boys, slipping and falling in their blood. *How can there be so much blood in people? How can they spill so much red liquid and still be alive?*

Stumbling, stumbling, limp arms brushing her sides and breasts, *Hurry! They're coming. The screams, Jesus, now they're howling. Have they set baboons on us or is it Satan himself? Holy Mary.* She couldn't remember the rest. The chills all over her, the limp arms flopping as they staggered in retreat. *Holy Mary, Holy Mary, Holy Mary.* Falling, thudding onto an unconscious male form, him groaning, she staggering to get up. *Sorry, sorry, I'm sorry.* His gurgling reply.

Men come out of the darkness, their hot musk thrilling her as they grabbed the wounded man and herself. Strong arms lifting her, setting her again on the journey. *Thank you*, she gasped, *Thank You* she kept repeating, following into the smoky blackness led only by the tug at the other end of the body. Stumbling, not falling, they were going inside now. Inside, and this was the new clinic, and look there's no blood on this floor just the housewife who lives here crossing herself, lips trembling, asking what she can do to help.

In her exhaustion there came a time when she was no longer afraid, even of death. The thousand guises she'd always worn, that surface she thought was her, fell away, and she was only a girl. Funny. Through it all she never felt like a woman, only a girl.

She saw it happen to the others as well. Then she understood her strength, her capability, her special kind of fearlessness. She saw she was brave without hating, kind without posturing, sensual without shame. She also felt a kind of love bloom within her. Love for her people, her nation, herself. A new kind of love born of a new kind of respect.

A certainty came to her as well. The sureness that she was fully capable of real love, and that the man upon whom she could bestow this gift was nearby. She could feel him, almost see and touch him. It was fate. He was coming to her and she was ready to meet him. When she did she would know. Maybe he wouldn't realize, might not understand, but she would. And that would be enough.

She had known frantic kissing, watched over by music pouring out of the dim yellow entrance to the dance. Had known boylust almost exploding in her arms. No, this would be none of that. It would be love and he would be a man. She knew that, believed in fate and in herself and when they met he too would believe. They only had to come together, she only had to ride the warm currents of her fate.

The bible said God knows even when a sparrow tumbles from the sky. So how could something as important as love, as miraculous as bringing a child into the world, not be a part of God's plan? It had to be so. It was simple and it simply had to be so.

There was something else Michaela knew. She understood that she and everyone around her were living in history. There had been a sudden upwelling of the earth, and all of them had been thrown about by that rising. And many had been consumed by the passions unleashed.

She knew that someday people would look back and study all of it. But her feelings were not ink congealing on a dry white page. She would not confuse her destiny with that which swirled around her.

For where was this revolution? How could you touch it and see it? So many calls to sacrifice, so many promises to be fulfilled just around the bend. To her it was like the wind. You could see the trees bend, the surface of the water change its hue, hear the whistle through bare branches. But where really, was the breeze? You could see the broken buildings, the smoke, the barbed wire and the empty chair at the table. But where was this thing everyone talked about, this revolution? And how would they know when it had arrived? Who would tell them this was the place, the moment, that this was justice?

She tried not to prejudge anyone, tried to maintain her soul in balance, keep her heart open, her words honest. She would not lose to the moment what could nurture her for a lifetime. You had to step back no matter what your cause. Even God rested on the seventh day.

Flaherty's was set close to the curbs of two intersecting neighborhood streets. It was a store for cigarettes, soda, crisps, fresh vegetables, and canned foods of all kinds. It was a five-aisled crossroads of the neighborhood. One of those places that had always been there.

Michaela did what she always did when she entered a room or place of business—she shifted the focus of the place to herself. It was just something that happened. No matter what they were doing, both men and women looked at her. Most smiled, some spoke, but always the room's center of gravity fell upon her until she released it with a touch, a glance, a self-depreciating remark. Then she took her place among the others, the hum of the day resumed, and but for furtive glances, the place was as before.

White apron folded short, the need for a cigarette hovering closer, a renegade wisp of hair hovering over her left eye, Michaela Murphy began this public part of her day.

Running her fingers over the worn green keys of the register, Michaela Murphy took in the form of the young man who had appeared on the street corner opposite. She saw Jimmy, both arms thrust into coat pockets, lift himself onto the balls of his feet, watched him stretch within his clothes, and then settle down to wait. His gaze went over the front windows of Flaherty's and she looked away, then glanced sideways to see him lighting a cigarette.

He looked so different than he had at the party held to honor him. He seemed younger, stronger, focused now on all around him. She had not spoken to him at the party, deliberately holding back, figuring he had enough well wishers. Then when he had fled, just before being introduced, she had had to bite her lips to stop the smile from spreading, for he had done exactly what she would have.

In that awkward moment when Louis had returned with the vanished guest of honor, her glance had briefly met Jimmy's, she trying to convey her feelings to him. *I know, I know, I hate crowds too. I know you see their thousand questions ready to cascade and smother. Tell us how they dragged you, tell us how they beat you, tell us how frightened you were, how alone, speak of your despair. Tell us, tell us, tell us. Please please please tell us.*

She'd seen it so many times in so many forms. The timid and the fearful ready to pick the marrow of the brave. And what were they seeking? Courage for themselves or cracks in the armor of those who stood firm when the mob ran?

Michaela knew all mobs eventually ran. Whether the tight

ring of cruel girls pushing the pretty one, the smart one, to the school wall, or those who never quite had the courage to stand up to the bully, to tell the cruel wit to stop. Michaela understood the rabble always fled, knocking one another over, to then gather on the next block, at the next class, after the meal. And always with words of what they had almost done, almost said, and what they were prepared to do next time.

As the crowd had closed back around Jimmy, Michaela wanted to call out what she knew, what she understood. That if you had bravery, when you stood apart, when you dared question when all others were mute, people wanted to pull you to pieces searching for what they lacked. And, she wanted to whisper, when they saw the pieces laid out, viewed the simple bravery of the daring boy, the terrible loneliness of the beautiful girl, when they understood there really was no secret, then they would turn on you.

Her thumb and forefinger squeezed the edge of the counter when she saw Jimmy Fitzgerald toss his cigarette away and stride toward the store entrance. Daring a quick breath, she gave him a smile as he entered, and he nodded, almost managing a smile in return, then dodged quickly down an aisle where, she could tell, his thoughts were fully focused on her.

Detective Ian MacDonald held the steering wheel with one hand, his coat unbuttoned so he could, if need be, grab the pistol in his belt with his free hand. Another gun was tucked beneath the dash where he could snatch it if gunfire forced him to drive while crouching down. He drove slowly past the row of houses, glancing down the cul-de-sac where he lived.

There was nothing unusual, and he made two rights that brought him behind the house where all seemed normal. Another right and back into the cul-de-sac, eyes front, glance bouncing off the rearview mirror. He stopped. He waited. Then he dared switch off the motor. He got out quickly.

Never fumble about, never duck down for that coin or package. Move quickly, surely. Use the car as cover if they surprise you. Don't dally. You can take all the detours in the world but the bastards still know you have to come home. And that's where they'll be waiting.

He strode quickly, his eyes locked on those of his wife who on was tiptoe peering through the small window of the bolted door. She would signal if there was a problem. She knew what to do, and she swung the door open an instant before he strode through it. She worked the locks and metal bars in seconds, then they embraced.

Nigel MacDonald bounded from the parlor.

"Ah, here's my wee man," said the detective.

The boy leaped to have his father swing him high and upsidedown. Nigel squealed with delight as his father hooked one arm behind the boy's knees and swung him gently, the joy and blood rushing to the youngster's face. Then he swung him to the floor, giving the child a quick tickle, producing squeals of delight.

"Now I'll be hearing all about your day," he said to the boy.

The little family went to the parlor where the boy recounted a walk to the bakery, a cat with orange stripes meowing in a tree, grocery shopping, and the marvel of counting backwards from ten.

"And how was Mummy's day? Can she count backwards too?"

"She can, Da, but I'm quicker."

Lauren MacDonald, 32, smiled, saying, "Oh he's a quick one alright." Then she asked, "And how was Da's day?"

He closed his eyes to all of it. Then blinked several times, the exhaustion beginning to hit him. For an instant he took her in, thinking. *God, how does she put up with it? How could I ever have got her into all of this? So strong, she's so strong.*

"Da's day was fruitful," he said. Then he grabbed his son lifting him high, turning him left and right. "Da had a fruitful day! Whatta ya think of that?"

"That's good, Da."

He lowered the boy, who scampered onto the small maroon couch. His wife went to the kitchen to mix him his drink. Scotch and soda, a single ice cube in a short thick glass. He nodded as he accepted it. Christ he was tired. His wrists ached, his knees too, his paperwork was spread to hell and gone. Then there were the meetings. One was scheduled for tomorrow morning first thing, and another the next morning, or was it the morning after?

You knew the men carrying the burden at these meetings. They came in looking a little bewildered, eyes red, deepset lines in the faces. They squinted around the room as though waiting for someone to explain to them what this bureaucratic mumbo-jumbo had to do with fighting the IRA.

And you knew the ones who carried only the load of ego and ambition. The ones who thrived in meetings and avoided the field. Crisp and alert, they snapped out charts and folders like honor guards executing salutes. How they lit up when the bosses spoke, following them around the place like goddamn poodles, all *yes sirs* and *no sirs*.

Of course it was those ones who would get all the big promotions. Then they could spew out more charts and proposals, all of which showed the struggle, at least the part on paper they had to answer for, was going swimmingly. *Yes sir, yes sir, just absolutely fucking brilliantly sir, and pay no attention to that gunman behind the curtain.*

"How's the drink?"

Detective MacDonald started, realizing he'd been daydreaming with the drink untouched in his hand. She smiled, he sipped.

"Just right, thanks."

She patted his shoulder and turned to the stove.

"We're almost ready," she said.

Ian got the boy, and at the table the trio bowed their heads and she said grace. As they ate they spoke of the cost of petrol and the weather. Then the boy would have his bath, yellow ducks would bob and soapy warm water would splash all over her. Her husband would watch the telly with its news, the volume low because she did not want to hear. Then the detective would go to his small room with its special telephone, his notebooks, and his reports. And she hoped, he would take out his collection of stamps and they would give him peace. Then the boy to bed, requests for stories and water, teddy bear and set the window shade just so.

Ian MacDonald stood in the dark bedroom listening to his wife's breathing, the rain dripping on painted sills, the patter of today's memories joining the river of all the days before.

After he had undressed for his shower he stood in the hallway that adjoined bedroom and bath, noting the distance to his pistol and the other gun in a downstairs closet. Always there, burned in a mind-map, so much a part of him he sometimes thought he should soap and rinse them as well. He used to bring a pistol within reach as he showered but had come to resent that last intrusion into his psyche. He would not be denied the simplicity of nakedness. *Christ, leave me some thread of what I once was. God grant me hot water and soap without snub-nosed death peeking through the steam.*

In ten minutes he was sliding beneath the sheets, shifting the day's events, letting the unnecessary drift off, keeping the nuggets of value, arranging, rearranging them, laying them out like weapons with which to smash the enemy.

The enemy. He preferred that term. He would not dignify them by using any of their words. The IRA, Provies, Stickies, The Rebels. Those words had the flat clatter of false coin. They were his enemy, not the people's, not the State's, they were his and his alone. The fear they caused permeated this place, was in the worn wood of every pub, was in the pavement, the air, the very red cells of the blood pumping in the people. The enemy. Damn them. The enemy. Damn them to hell.

God put people on earth for a reason. Many people never learned that, but he understood. God had put him here, in this country, in this time, for one reason. He was to defeat the enemy.

Yes he loved his wife, yes he loved his son. But that was a separate thing. That was human, that was natural. Congealed inside his chest was something else. Neither love nor hate, coiled so deep in him the currents of his soul flowed around it. That was this mission God had bestowed. He was to defeat the enemy. He was justified to use any means, any methods, because he was privy to this special knowledge. He touched them, he listened to them, he beat them and hugged them, he broke them and made them whole again.

And he knew a secret. While the world watched, while millions argued and debated, while thousands of soldiers trained and deployed, this war was waged by a precious few. Whether chosen or cursed, these few, on both sides, were a fulcrum, a simple machine whose tilting would pour them all to either civilization or savagery.

He was eight years old when he first became aware of Catholics. He had been sitting in the back seat of the family car, the only child, his place in the world set by the twin pillars of his parents. Now as they rode he sensed a tension spring up in his parents, a sudden silence. Amid the chatter with his wife, David MacDonald had made a wrong turn. The houses they passed by were sunken, sullen, dirty, like the men on the street corners staring at the polished vehicle coasting past. No Union Jacks snapped proudly in the breeze, no women busied themselves with sweeping clean sidewalks, no one watered flower boxes on windowsills.

Abruptly his father stopped, turned, and rapidly retraced their journey, his mother's hand at her throat, the men on the sidewalk unmoving as they flashed by, unmoving and staring, staring as the little boy realized his father was running away. His father was running from this dirty sullen place, these men who stood so still with their long stares. The anxiety in his parents jumped to the little boy as they fled.

When they found familiar streets the adults relaxed, Father made a joke, Mother chuckled a bit too hard, and none of them mentioned again what had transpired. The parents thought the boy had been unaware of their accidental intrusion into a Catholic neighborhood. But he had seen and he had felt and something of him had locked onto what had transpired and would never let it go.

He was a boy who loved order. His toys had to be arranged in perfect rows, his rock collection labeled and placed neatly onto shelves. Later his plans for life were set like a set of stairs for him to walk up. He wanted order and a policeman brought order, he sought control, and the policeman must be obeyed.

Young Ian MacDonald enjoyed a challenge, a difficult task, as long as he had all the pieces on hand to do the job. The law would be the tools he used, he would build and protect with British propriety and the firm Ulster hand. His father had imbued the boy with that ethic. When all else failed, remember the firm Ulster hand. Discipline, strict adherence to the rules, proper diction, proper clothing, proper morals, proper man.

Some men, his father would explain, lacked these important qualities. They were weak in morals, quick to violence, undisciplined, misguided. And, the boy was reminded, dangerous. His father didn't mention who these dangerous men were. For the boy had seen their streets, their dingy houses, their nicotine stained fingers and piercing eyes, had grown to fear their throbbing offspring bursting forth like the blown seeds of a thousand fertile fields.

Catholics. How seldom the word was mentioned in the MacDonald household. Once the boy had announced a clever phrase he'd read. *All roads lead to Rome.* After a silence in which his father's disappointment in him echoed off the walls, Mister MacDonald put a hand on the boy's shoulder.

"We don't say that here," he whispered. And it was never

said there again.

Ian came to accept the simple division and his world of small privileges. He understood his family had a lovely garden in a tidy yard, they had an automobile, they went on holiday to a lake. The Catholics lacked these things, did not keep their homes tidy. His family and neighbors worked hard. The Catholics did not. He prayed to God. The Catholics worshipped the Pope in Rome. His family did that which was moral and correct. The Catholics could sin over and over and had only to confess to wipe their slate clean.

He became a police officer, and a very good one. Every so often there was a flare-up. A donnybrook, the Catholics called it. Fists and bottles flying, batons cracking skulls with a righteous hollow ring. And it would end. And everyone would return to their pubs and homes.

He married, and their little boy was two when the Catholics started their civil rights marches. Illegal marches, Irish women shouting the vilest things at police officers, then singing *We Shall Overcome.* And they pushed and pushed and the police pushed back and this thing that was inside everyone, this proper arrangement that was as it had always been, exploded.

It stunned them all. Fire bombings, hijackings, looting, arson. The world turned upside down, day and night all become one deafening piercing scream. The look of terror on the faces of the young policemen. Ian wondering, *God, does my face look that way? Are my eyes that wide-white?*

The sudden realization that they were losing. Being pushed back. Then the calling up of the B-specials. The reserves. Any man who could swing a baton, or throw a tear gas grenade or a punch. Those men going amok. Riding on armored cars shooting Catholics, frothing at the mouth, berserk with hatred. He'd gone up to them, yelled into their faces, grabbed hold of their arms telling them to stop. Until they turned their rage on him.

And Officer Ian MacDonald had to back away and to pretend he did not see.

He was Dorothy riding the tornado, but there would be no Oz, no wizard, and this being Belfast, the film was in color and black and white all at the same time.

He was going mad. His tongue was swollen to the roof of his mouth, tear gas seeped into his stomach, he was bleeding, he was almost deaf, he was filthy, his clothes reeked, his body stank, and again he and his fellow officers understood. Despite all men on duty, despite the B-specials, they were being ground down. That night the sound of gunfire from near a church. It was not fellow officers, it was not the B-Specials. They had looked at one another when they realized the gunfire was coming from the Catholic side.

The myths had sprung from the ground and were howling at them, the ghosts of everything repressed by court and boot was loose in the city. The IRA had shoved aside its coffin lid and was striding the dark streets. A tidal wave of energy drenched the Catholics, their songs were made flesh, their impotent rage suddenly had form, they shouted to their dead fathers: *Look, we are become men!*

Ian MacDonald felt the ground beneath him vanish, and he fell into black space. The blackness sucked his strength, desires, energy, identity, so that he could barely follow orders, let alone issue them. There could be no firm Ulster hand if there was nothing to stand upon, nothing to see, no strength if every move sent you spinning in a weightless void.

Then the Protestant people rose up, attacking Catholics *en masse.* Burning them out. Running them south to their papist haven.

At last the British Army arrived. Crisp, clean, overpowering them all, making the Catholics back away and the policemen feel ashamed.

And it stopped, for a time. Time enough for each fighter to

stagger to his corner and be repaired, encouraged to look into what had made him a man, to put both hands into that liquid, splash it on his face and drink it deeply, then come to the center of the ring a wounded raging entity of song, shame, law, religion, fear and pride.

Ian MacDonald had become someone he would have shrunk from a month before. Without referee or rule book the two sides again closed upon one another, embracing, pummeling, biting into one another's wounds, and neither would go down, neither would back away, neither could stop.

In that pause Ian MacDonald became something new. Never again would he allow himself to lose control, never again would he be without an interior compass. He washed and washed and still felt the stink of sweat and panic that had been on him. He ordered new uniforms and still did not feel quite clean. *Yes*, he thought, *I am dirty. But the enemy lives in filth and I must roll in that filth to contain him.* And he felt always the fear. He would use that fear to focus. He would use the enemy's own weapon to defeat him.

Detective Ian MacDonald settled at his desk of grey metal and stubborn drawers. He looked about the room. The younger men had the advantage of not having known normality. He allowed a single glance around the room thinking, *They are distorted in a distorted world. Perhaps that is evolution, never experiencing the disadvantage of reason.*

The detective stretched in his chair, feeling the passing years, the slight paunch, the little aches. *How ironic,* he thought, *the more you fight them the less time you have to stay in shape. The very act of fighting makes you weaker, vulnerable. Don't think that. Don't think at all. Just act.*

And the detective carried another burden. He bore the weight of every father, son, wife, daughter, sister and brother, grandmother and grandfather he had informed of the death of a loved one. Ian MacDonald unconsciously put his right hand over his solar plexus, to that region where the memories twisted and chafed. Where lay the memories of probing at the limp forms slapped by gunfire. He took in the carnage of the car bomb, the legs, shoes with feet in them tossed far from the person they carried through life. He listened to the dentist carefully explain the similarities of an old x-ray and what lay on the examining table.

Then he stood before a small house, inside a family going about its family routine, a family he was about to smash into a thousand pieces. He pushed through his dread, forcing one step after another like a deep sea diver salvaging misery. Sometimes they were hunched in a knot, all of them, for they knew.

Then he confirmed the awful news and they fell into his arms and he felt their souls meld with his own. Or they screamed and cursed, chased him away as he tried to calm them.

And the worst time. An IRA bomb going off in a car prematurely. A muffled *whumph* of white smoke and brown dust sweeping the sidewalk clean, the blood of the dead creating a red Rorschach test on a cement wall. He had spent hour after hour at the scene. Then on to the homes. *Your wife and child are gone sir. Your husband is dead. Your mummy and daddy are no more. Your sister is deceased, your brother obliterated.*

Fifteen hours into it he knocked on a red door with lovely yellow flowers in a nearby window box and then his mind went blank. He'd left his notebook in the car and he could not remember who was dead and who was about to open the door.

"Jesus." Was all he managed as the woman's footsteps came closer. But she knew. Thank God for that.

"It's my William, isn't it?"

He could only nod.

"Please come in, Sir."

The woman whose name he'd forgotten spoke of her husband of 32 years and he'd asked how she spelled her last name. And then he remembered.

Never had he hated the enemy so much as that day. Never had he felt such guilt, felt such a failure. All the victims, and all those who loved them, held fingers tight around his ribcage, wanting in wanting out. They were all there as he promised that the ones who did this would be found. And he knew they would not, knew they fed on this death and despair and it made them stronger while he sat at his desk reading forms and filing them, creeping into middle age.

Now he ate his sandwich wrapped in white paper while they connected their wires and timers, molded their gelignite and Semtex and their energy grew and grew. *Don't think, he reminded himself, don't think, just act.*

And he would act. As long as he was a man he would struggle, even if they killed him. He would not be defeated as long as he struggled. And that Ian MacDonald would always do. He would struggle against the enemy and love his wife and little boy, and one day he would triumph. One day the storm would end. Perhaps abruptly, perhaps it would pad away on the paws of the ancient mist that brought it.

Then the people would emerge from their shelters, blinking in the newly blue sky and they would see him and the other chosen ones standing tall. Then the people would understand, the world would see. That was what he lived for. That and his little boy running like a fawn to greet his daddy in a world of order. Then with his wife by his side he would swing the boy and hold him aloft to the wind and the whole world.

Filing that vision away, the policeman turned back to his work.

In the dark they settled almost to sleep, and the house settled into itself as well. Lauren MacDonald's fingernails gently rubbed her husband's neck and hair, crossing and recrossing, tracing the depths of her feelings for him.

She knew he was still awake but almost taken by sleep, and she allowed her mind to wander. Gifted with the ability to lock bad things away, she focused only on the pleasant. She imagined having another child, a little girl, all dressed in pretty clothes and visiting Grandma and Grandpa. And she saw her son growing tall and strong, a fine young man coming home from university.

Then to her favorite bit of imagining—what to do if they won the Irish Sweeps. All the bills paid and a fine summer house on the ocean, facing west to the wild Atlantic. She would hang clean sheets in the Atlantic breeze and wrap her family in them every night. And they would own a sturdy little black Scotty dog that would run loose and free on the sands. He would be a happy little fellow, all confidence and sharp as a tack.

Then she moved on to the favorite part of her dream. Reaching back to childhood to find lost friends and pay their debts and give them enough to start out all new in life. And the people in the neighborhood who had financial needs, she'd help them too. She'd arrange family reunions and fly relatives in from around the world. And the meals would be catered and everyone would receive a small tasteful gift.

She and Ian would buy a beautiful new house, and she could see every room and exactly what piece of furniture would go where. She could see paintings on the walls and the color of every rug and the pattern of every dish. She'd help poor families, set up scholarships, train young people for skilled jobs and overseas study.

Eventually word of her good works would spread in proper circles and she would be called to London. There in Buckingham Palace the Queen would make her Lady Lauren, and Lady Lauren would walk from the room nodding ever so slightly to proper applause, her proud family all about. She could almost feel the gown she would wear that day, as sleep embraced her and her hand slid noiselessly down to her husband's shoulder.

Careful not to wake her, he took the hand in his as he eased from his side to his back. Then he pressed her hand to the mattress and lay still. He listened. There was nothing. He listened to that. All was still, as if the house itself were holding a finger to its lips so as to hear better.

She sighed. He pulled the sheet a little higher on her shoulder, thinking, *someday it will end. Someday, somehow, it will end. God let me see that day.* He tried to believe it would end, pressed his eyes tighter trying to imagine it, but could not. It felt like the time he was thirteen, his family at a lake, and he decided to swim alone to an island in the lake's center.

He set out, face in the water, up for a breath, face down again, sure as youth. The island was there, not getting bigger, then it was drifting, drifting, sideways and seemingly back. In the cold water he felt the sudden warm pump of his heart and he paused to look to the beach. Gasping at its distance, he momentarily flailed in the water, too far to go back, too far to the island.

He wanted to cry, to screech for help, to shout of the unfairness of such extreme consequences of such a small choice. He fought his panic and floated, resting, gently kicking his legs back to the beach, wanting to cry and scream all at once. Cold pools of water from the deep startled his legs, mocking him as did the delighted cries of children on the sand. And very slowly, very deliberately he dog-paddled, floated and swam back to the muddy shallows of life. He was alive but defeated—and worse, humiliated.

He never told anyone about that swim, not even Lauren. But he swore he would not make that mistake again. Never would he underestimate a challenge or an enemy. Never again would he throw anything precious to fate's uncaring maw.

But now he was in the lake again. The start of the violence so far back, the end nowhere to be seen as they all struggled and the water tried to pull them under.

A noise. Like a tapping. Outside or in? Couldn't tell. He tensed, looking to the holster on the nightstand, looking at Lauren lost to dreams. He waited for the sound to repeat. It was rare they came at night. Now his heart joined the vigil, pump-pump, pump-pump, blood-heat spilling through him, pushing out as pinpricks of sweat. *Damn!* he thought. *Damn.*

Get up? *No wait, you'll scare her.* Pump-pump. Swallow, once then twice. He slid off the bed, grabbing the holster, turning to see her still undisturbed.

Check the boy. *He's fine, those are my silent steps on the carpet. The alarm has two backup systems. We're safe.* Pump-pump.

He edged down the stairs and through the dark house, watching for motion, listening for a creak or a breath. He went through the rooms, his left hand on the outside of the holster, right on the gun butt. *Damn them to hell. Damn them all.*

From darkened windows he checked the street, the yard, the neighbors' yards. All quiet. He stared at the car, telling himself to do an extra-careful inspection in the morning. *That might upset her. Well, it can't be helped. Better upset than a widow.*

He stood at the kitchen sink. Putting the holster down he pressed his hands together then poured a little water from the tap. Just enough to slake what this incident brought to his throat.

He rinsed the glass and put it upside down next to the sink.

Upstairs he checked the boy again, put the weapon where it had been, and slid in next to his wife, who sighed a dreamy welcome and touched his side. He lay still, listening, his heart occasionally giving an extra beat of readiness. He listened for a long time. He didn't check his watch but it was very late before sleep came and he went to his familiar dream of bus stations and trains.

In his dream he had to get home, but there was no connection. And he rode and ran through stations and streets. And a little man in a booth kept reappearing to tell him he must be mistaken. Detective MacDonald would insist, shouting into the booth, *no, I know this place, they've changed things a bit, the stairs, the entrance ways, but I know the walls, I know this station's name!* Sometimes he could see the little man's face and sometimes not. And the words came right out of the little man's head, thoughts that could be heard. And always he would smile and say the same thing. "It's the confusion, Sir, now please move on."

And he did move on, to indecipherable station names, departing trains, empty idling busses. And he ran, his tie too tight, his shirt soaking in sweat, but always he came back again. And always the little man in his tiny dark booth repeated his mantra.

When the soldiers ran, their boots made pleasant splashes of sound on sidewalk and street. One by one the young men dashed forward, doorway to doorway. One would sprint with rifle held chest-high, then the next man rushed up a sidewalk or across an intersection. They were melded to their SLR rifles, as if the weapons were pulling at their arms as they dragged the soldiers across Belfast's scarred face, yanking them back into Ireland's past where everything present resided.

The soldiers' breathing was controlled, their eyes white-wide, sucking in windows, vehicles, doorways, ruddy faces, tumbling litter, dogs, kids, mumbling winos, the shouting crazed. They saw two youths their own age, standing still and breathing the vapors of colorless hate. It all came in and illuminated their minds with a stabbing unblinking light, hurting their eyes. Their heads throbbed, their moist fingers slid on the rifle's unyielding contours. But the soldiers kept running forward, doorway to doorway, street to street.

If one was very close and dared to look, the patrol was a freeze-frame of expressions—fear, anger, bewilderment, bemusement, loathing, determination, pride, awkwardness. Some of their eyes screamed *I'll kill you,* the furtive glances of others cried *this is not my fault.* And then with all the soft sounds they made chasing them, they were gone.

The sniper thought, *such things there are to see in the silent movie of the rifle's crosshairs.* There were children playing games of tag, men rolling kegs of Guinness into pubs, British armored cars clawing their way up little streets, peoples' lives lived pressed behind the glass of little windows. Men fixing cars, a dog giving his opinion of things with a leg raised to a wall, women preparing midday meals, and always children. There were children everywhere. They were in pairs, in groups, piled upon one another, sprawled in the dirt and playing on pavement.

Sometimes there were special treats in this silent world. A row of rooftop flowers bowing to the passing breeze, a boy stealing a kiss on a corner, the girl's hands on his chest in mock recoil. It was all here in this hushed world with the thin black crosshairs at its heart.

He breathed out. How erotic this was. He breathed in. He was deep within the building. He had his own set of stairs, his own wooden railings, he was in what had been a bedroom. There was a nice hole in the wall, and the wall beyond had another hole. That hole went through a closet presenting a view through a shattered window.

All so lovely. He breathed. He listened to his heart. He flexed his fingers, once then twice very slowly. He waited. He didn't mind waiting. Not for a film or a girl, not for a train or for the sun to touch the horizon. Waiting was part of the journey.

His fingers caressed the rifle. A Lee Enfield .303. A weapon of World War I, a gun that many an army would scoff at. However, the sniper knew it was not obsolete any more than an aged wine was obsolete. It was proven, it was etched in history. Young men now old had held this weapon and he could feel their souls in its smooth stock, could see the Hun scurrying his last moments into its sights on the moonscape of Flanders.

No, this weapon was not obsolete, and would not be until boys stopped climbing trees and searching for buried treasure, until they no longer cared what was around a river's bend.

His judo instructor had taught him to use the momentum of his opponent's attack to his own advantage. His professors had taught him that often the answer was right in front of you, if you were clever enough to see, patient enough to connect, determined enough to dare.

He breathed out, he breathed in, and he waited within the cloistered world of the scope. There. He saw it. Something, something, just there, He focused. A soldier's face peeked around a corner in the quiet distance. The soldier sprinted diagonally across to a doorway. They would all follow, like little ducks behind their mother. He breathed out. See, there was another, thinking it must be safe if the man before him made it. He kept the crosshairs on the doorway and they kept coming into view.

He knew it would be a 12-man patrol and he counted until the sixth man. That would split them nicely in two. They would be strung out and screaming. Should they go forward or back? Who had been hit? Where is the sniper? Screaming and screaming. He was glad they were too far away to hear. He hated it when people were loud.

The sixth man came into perfect focus. Dust jumped into the air of the bedroom, just as the soldier stepped into the bullet, both his feet going up, his back hitting the wall behind him, and he crumbled to a seated position, going instantly and unnervingly still. The soldier's comrades shouted and his wristwatch ticked on without him, as the sniper calmly collected his tools and slipped away.

The soldiers, all but one, were screaming. The children were racing home, and even the people close to the shooter had no idea where the shot had come from. Reinforcements poured into the area, streets were blocked, men were slammed against walls, doors were kicked in to reveal little children cowering.

The sniper walked down the street with his left hand in his pocket, his right swinging to the tune he whistled. He bought a newspaper and a little cellophane package of cashew nuts. He walked past the little park, past a pub while he checked his watch. There now, the bus was right on time. Right on time to carry him downtown, where they would search him at the security gates and again at the door of the bookstore, where he would linger among the stacks of knowledge.

Captain James Cross rapped on the narrow wooden door, waited for a response that did not come, then slowly pushed the door open. The man on the bed had both feet on the floor, his head down, his hands clasped, and did not look up as the captain entered.

"It wasn't your fault, Sergeant," said the captain.

Sergeant Albert Roberts raised his gaze. He had not been crying. His expression was pushed deeper into grief than tears.

"He was my man, Sir."

"He was, Sergeant, I know. But nothing could have prevented it. The gunman was near a half-a-mile off."

The captain slid onto the small metal chair near the sergeant's folding desk. He was six months older than the man before him, but had always taken comfort in the sergeant's ancient wisdom. Neither ever acknowledged it, but theirs was a father son relationship occasionally inconvenienced by rank.

"The police have specialists," said the captain. "They can triangulate from where the round hit Private Madison. Can pinpoint the sniper's position. We'll get him."

"I never heard the shot, Sir." The sergeant spoke without moving.

"I know, Sergeant."

"Even after the boy fell. I didn't hear the shot. That's no amateur out there, that was no lucky round, Sir."

Captain Cross glanced at the wire mesh waste bin by the desk. Crumpled papers nearly filled it, the flailing efforts, he knew, of the sergeant trying to write a letter of condolence to English parents. The captain raised his voice.

"Battalion's gone over every detail, every movement of the patrol. It was all correct, not a misstep. You're in no way to blame."

"Yes, Sir."

The captain told him there would be extra patrols tomorrow. He thought it best to keep the men active. The day after there would be a memorial service for Private Madison.

"Would you care to speak at the service, Sergeant?"

The man on the bed slowly stood, ran his hands down his shirt, set his stare on the captain and said, "I would, Sir."

The two exchanged a salute and the captain left. When the door closed the sergeant folded back down, then leaned back against the wall. Though he had prayed, he did not feel the hand of God in any of it. Though he had not wept, he was mourning. Though he had no words, he would speak for the dead. He looked at the empty chair then whispered,

"He was my man, Sir. He was my man and I lost him."

Out of the rifle's scope and into this room like a swimmer emerging from down deep, ears held tight by water, lusting for the surface. The sniper broke into noise, white clouds, cool air, sucking in life in one violent gasp, killing the air to live. Alive. He was alive and the other was not. He was sprawled on a bed staring at a ceiling, and the other stared at what only he could know. Maybe nothing, maybe everything all at once. He liked that, everything all at once and forever.

This event, in his thoughts each crack of the rifle was an event, had been very clean. He knew they would not come for him, had not a clue who he was. He stood and as always, he washed, slowly, correctly, drying carefully, allowing the event to be stored, to be framed and set into its surroundings. They taught him that in the army. Stay focused, stay aware, focus, then focus again. They're all around you. Keep your weapon clean, keep your body clean. Focus.

From a quadrant of the sky outside he heard the deep pulse of a helicopter blade, heard its metal thumping, a mad woman beating a sky rug. The bass notes ran away and back, a frantic dog on a leash as below soldiers thrashed the neighborhoods trying to flush out the sniper. They would fail, but they and their war bird succeeded in jarring loose pieces of his memory.

Nothing brought back his first love like the aerial mantra of an H1, the Huey, pure sex against a blue sky, the balls-tingling plunges to a landing zone under fire, the wet-kiss joy of heading back to base alive in the arms of your beastly grinning buddies. He missed it so.

Again he remembered his first time killing. Inside a Huey, the helicopter bouncing off the rising air of the paddies like a speed boat over lake waves. *Whumph*, and they all bent at the waist, arms outstretched to the prisoner, leaning into his emaciated form. *Whump*, and their arms snaked up in unison, ballerinas in green fatigues, waiting for their male lead to command the stage. Which he did, three stripes glowering on his arms, and at one GI in particular, set just apart from the others, the soldier wishing all of this away. Himself.

"Joe College."

He whispered it, or did he just mouth the words?

"Joe College."

The squad's fingers rested on the bound prisoner. It had to be all or none. So their sergeant repeated his mantra.

"Joe College."

And the reticent soldier joined his hand to the prisoner, felt the boy's heart pounding, felt its beats in five fingertips where it joined the racing protests of his own. The boy locked his eyes on the reluctant soldier. The one who had found him in his little spider hole, the one who had pulled him gently into the sunlight, the one who kept whispering to him, reassuring the trembling Communist that he would not be harmed, the one who bound his hands behind his back then offered a cigarette to young lips trembling in the heat of Asia's summer. That one.

The communist watched as his captor's honor evaporated under the sergeant's glare, his comrades' evaluations, God's wide eye. When they all had their hands on him the kid knew. They were going to throw him out.

And they did. He was there and he was gone. But one of his sandals stayed. Right there just outside the door, staring back at the bug-eyed GIs. Maybe it wanted to be their friend. Maybe it would follow them home. Maybe it would testify against them. Then it flashed away to find its owner, and the five men exhaled.

Later it was the sandal they talked about. *The flying sandal, damn thing was haunted, stay away from THAT paddy man. Bad karma, bad vibes, bad day, bad omen. Stay away, stay way the hell away.*

That was his turning point. Five nights later, peering through a star scope, he saw little green men making their way toward him and his sleeping comrades. He shot them, jolting the platoon awake to confirm three dead VC sappers. To bask in the platoon's adulation.

"Didn't say nothin'.

"Just popped 'em."

"Hard corps."

"Dead eye."

"Arctic cold."

"Silent as a monk."

And he became Monk. A new name like a new shirt. He wore it and it looked good and everybody was happy. Three nights later he repeated his performance with the star scope, this time dispatching two thirds of an enemy mortar crew as they crept out of a tree line. The others blessed him. They touched him for good luck. A week later he realized the local VC were marking booby trapped trails with three small stones, causing his comrades to declare they would name their children after him.

For the first and only time he was where he belonged. Here he could face his fears because all fear in this place was physical. The boy who had enlisted still terrified of a dark cellar moved smoothly through black jungle. The one who had leaped up at the touch of a mosquito now settled into the world of insects, appreciating them, holding still at their frantic probes, lying comfortably in the slime of their world to kill his fellow man.

And he got very good at that. So good they gave him the company's sniper rifle. So good they made the new guys carry his gear. That good, that intimate, that alive, that revered. Then his time was up and they sent him home. Awkward handshakes amid sandbags and warm beer. They said how they envied him, his leaving, lucky bastard. He couldn't speak because something was being torn from him, something he loved, and he knew he would never find it again.

All alone and terribly frightened he came home to Boston. To stare at the Charles River and the coeds sprawled along its banks, to seek answers for what he had done, who he had been, in the bookstores of Harvard Square. To drink beside his intellectual superiors and ask their opinions, which were legion.

They explained he had been a dupe, a pawn, damaged goods, a war criminal, a murderer, he hated his daddy or his mummy. They explained he was afraid of women, of intimacy, of being homosexual, of being a rapist, of being castrated. He should have gone to Canada, or jail, or grad school, or taught school.

On weekends their wisdom was not available because they were on the Vineyard or Nantucket. But they always came back tanned and rested, once suggesting he stand before one of their committees to accept a group reprimand. He thought they were joking and had laughed out loud. But the lords of morals were serious.

After that they met him with silence and trust fund smirks. He was shunned with learned quotes, French phrases, and names that were dropped just so. Soon he went back across the Charles, back to three-deckers, pool tables, juke boxes and fist fights. Back where he'd come from.

But in his heart he wanted to be one of them. Rich, smooth-skinned, poised, brilliant, armed with an array of quips and *bon mots* at his fingertips. With a beautiful mom and an accomplished dad. To be comfortable in his skin, instead of frantic and stumbling, frightened by the pronunciation of wines and appetizers, paralyzed by the array of silverware. He so longed to stop being afraid, or to just know what caused the unfocused fear. To find an end to having to appear in the stadium and run the high hurdles blindfolded every day.

As he left their world he knew that at most his pouring out of his heart would become an anecdote at dinner, a sop to their argument for world peace. The sacred nicknames of fallen comrades would cross their lips. Just one more betrayal for him, one more thing that pulverized grunts and a scrawny VC would lay on him in the hereafter.

So he drank to what tunes three quarters in a slot would bring, he slept with girls who blew smoke rings above the sheets, he worked jobs he hated and that hated him. He came to realize how much his country needed movement, any movement, in order to stand itself. The helicopter assaults, bullets and bombs thudding into the earth as young warriors leaped forth, killing and being killed for a hill they would then abandon.

At home he stared in disbelief at a scheme in his city to make equality tangible by forcing black and white school kids out of their own schools onto busses and throwing them into enemy neighborhoods. He saw the whites flee the city, the blacks rage at a thousand insults real and imagined. Saw the suburbanites *tsk tsk* at it all while remaining morally indignant, deeply sympathetic and completely unscathed. The faraway and well-to-do declared themselves pure. Anyone could see it was the Irish in the city who were guilty. Hell, they were primitives. The suburbanites were sure of that because their newspaper told them so.

Through it all he drank, he sat in his room cleaning his rifle, he waited for the race war he was sure was imminent, but it never came.

Later he realized it was all a dance. The blacks stepped forward, the whites stepped back, the blacks took two steps the whites did a twirl. White neighborhoods became black, a slum area became full of lofts and dreadfully sensitive white professionals. One two three, one two three, and turn. An eighteenth century minuet, all that was needed was powdered wigs and gowns. Maybe the suburbanites' ancestors had passed them down, wigs and gowns, maybe they were kept at summer homes, and perhaps they were worn during that long commute into Boston.

He watched and he withdrew, working nights, sleeping days. He read, he walked the city. And missed his love, War, more and more. He longed for the kindness, the generosity, the honesty of it all. And he watched another conflict grow in Ireland, the land of his parents. Saw the faces like looking in a mirror. He watched and read, watched and read, always feeling the pull of that ancient place. It could make him alive again, he was sure of it. This ancient race had a collective subconscious and he was part of it, could in dreams sip from that deep well.

The Irish did not move. They never left a neighborhood, never let go of an offense, until it had turned into hatred. They stood still and let it wash over them, let it burn and brand them, then they shouted to the world who they were.

In Belfast hatred was natural, primordial, in the open, to be embraced, nurtured and worn. It was life, and he knew Belfast would make him alive, would love him and tell him it understood. He had to go there. He had to see the men and hear the sounds. He had to gasp air tinged with cordite, he had to drive himself to the surface and gulp in that atmosphere. He had to go there.

He moved easily through Boston and its bars—listening, acknowledging, confiding and understanding. And he learned as he listened. Most of what he heard was beer-talk. But he patiently sifted through the words, the hints and nods, until he found the steady gaze, the lack of bravado, the gallows humor. He saw it in the *other* and the *other* saw in him, and they gave him information and he bought an airplane ticket.

These were his people. Though their tongues bent differently around the language, their streets looked like an amusement park's maze, their views almost mad, he knew he was one of them. He could see it.

He had always seen things first. But all he could do was see them. He saw what girls wanted, saw they wished for a story and a song. Understood that somehow they could shut their hearts off from their minds and hear only the false words, see only the calculated gestures thrown into their girl nights like July sparklers.

In high school he perceived the jerk and his ego on their appointed rounds, watched the beauties grow ripe amid the jerk's fields. A watering of words, a sudden needless cruel jibe, a gift of flowers, an imitation of precious stone, false gold, false love, false boy, and he had her.

But he himself could not do it. He was like a camera that could focus to just a point and then all became blur. And the girls saw this and mocked him, saw this and drifted away, held tight by the ones who only wanted to take.

He heard himself when the DJ played songs of the lonely, the wronged, and when he was old enough to drive he was cocooned in glass and metal on rainy neon streets. And on those dark nights he saw and saw and could affect none of it. Now he was here in this Irish conflict and it was correct. What he did was honest. The enemy was armed and alert. It was fair.

The adrenalin flowed from him and he stared at the cool pale green paint of the wall.

He liked to remember – far, far back. He liked to recall being a little boy. Someone once told him that healthy people feel the world, sick people feel their bodies. He was a little boy who felt the world, felt the rain dripping from green leaves pass through him, felt the magic of man's machines heaving snow from Boston streets, and trains thundering from the city pulling freight cars that danced in joy to the horizon.

They told him he was odd. Weird. Smart weird. Scary smart. *Kid, you think too much. Kid, you read too much.* And they were furious at him. *Terrible grades and so intelligent. A disgrace. Buckle down. Get going young man, produce.*

He pressed his face with two hands to all of that. No, he must think of the future. He must plan beyond all of this, look far down the road, imagine what lay beyond that curve.

He would stop if he met a woman. If she would hold him close, touch cool fingers to his warm skin he would stop. If she would listen to everything he was and was not, and still hold him close he would stop. But there was no such woman and never would be.

So he had to persevere. He had to imagine her, and that would be enough. To imagine was almost to love, he knew that. And he imagined, and she understood perfectly and that was enough. And that would always be enough, and the future would become the past and he would watch and see it all, stay ever inward with his secrets and plans, and God would see and only God would understand. That and the crack of the rifle would be enough for now.

The growing tension in the room pushed the three men into a tighter circle, pressed the cloud of cigarette smoke tighter around them, made it stale, choking any pleasure from fresh drags. There were no jokes, no words, each man in the room was standing on a small circle and all around that circle was an abyss and no one could acknowledge that.

Louis pressed the black ski mask that was stuffed into his jacket pocket. Jimmy tried not to think, tried to see himself after this operation having a beer.

Tommy Higgins, the driver, stared at the floor. Higgins was 20, quietly brave, intense, at five-foot-ten tall for a Belfast man. He could handle action, but this period of not knowing terrified him, his hands shook. At this point his voice, if he dared speak, would quake.

The intelligence man came in again and for the last time went over what they already knew. The Brits, as all people will do, had fallen into a little routine. They were leaving the barracks on Royal Avenue in two jeeps at the same time every morning. Had been doing so for over a week. Two jeeps, four Brits. "Like they're out for a lark," said the intelligence man.

A small bomb was waiting in a car at Grosvenor Avenue and Ross Street. It would be set off by a wire tripped by an IRA man. They didn't need to know who he was and they didn't want to know. They would wait for the explosion, then rush the survivors. The intelligence man repeated the instructions.

"Keep firing, aim low, pick your target. Then get out of there."

The IRA car would be dumped and burned. They would get into a second car and zoom off, leaving weapons and masks in that car, then rally at the safe house.

Questions? None were asked. Especially not the one dangling in everyone's head. *What if the jeeps were bait? What if Special Air Services were lying in wait for them?*

The SAS, the elite of the British military. Men who seemed to rise from the fucking ground to murder, then disappear like smoke. Ruthless, crack shots, deadly with knives or bare hands. The SAS were the tip of a very broad sword stretching back to London, a sword that existed to kill men just like the three in this room. An international killing mechanism aimed at men who had never been out of Belfast. But that was one point in the Irishmen's favor, because after all, this was Belfast.

And a further element was in play. There were scouts about on foot and in vehicles. And there was another gun car with three men just like themselves who would not participate unless things went to hell. Going to hell, they knew, would be a trip of seconds not minutes. If this was a trap the other unit might as well be in Dublin. Or, as Louis summed up the other team to the intelligence man, "tits on a bull."

In the car the three clasped hands, gave one shake and pushed on. Balaclavas were on laps, Armalite rifles atop the masks, eyes going left and right like strobes, fingers drumming, shaking, drumming, shaking, shaking. Everyone's mouth feeling like they'd licked the day's lesson off the blackboard.

They parked. Louis was next to the driver, Jimmy alone in the back, when *Jesus here they came 20 fucking minutes early.* Masks on, rifle safeties off.

"OK!" screamed Louis.

They crouched down, then the *whump* of the explosion felt more than heard. Jumping out, Jimmy saw a jeep on its side, two inert forms pushed to the windscreen as the other jeep flashed out of the smoke on two wheels, and he turned to shoot at it. It righted itself, almost flipped in the other direction as his rifle kicked into his shoulder, and that jeep was gone.

Louis, on one knee, was firing at the forms in the glass. *Bapbapbap*, he stood. *Bapbapbap.* Jimmy joined him, a short burst, another, and another.

Louis was running back to their car. He shouted. Jimmy, who now ran the other way toward the overturned jeep, didn't respond. Someone screamed Jimmy's name, but the shouts were bouncing off him. He only knew he had to get to the soldier in the jeep. Again he felt the soldiers' punches and kicks. They were laughing at him, he was naked and small and they were laughing. He could hear the bastards laughing, and he cursed as he reached the jeep.

Ripping the door open, he grabbed the uniform then pulled the inert form out. Took the man under the arms and half ran, half stumbled to the car, shoving the soldier at the back seat, slipping and falling onto the man's legs then grabbing his boots and folding him up onto the seat. Somewhere Louis was screaming, and Tommy Higgins was turned around, eyes wide, hands frozen at the wheel.

"What the fuck are ya doin? What the fuck are ya doin?" Louis screamed as Jimmy shoved and pushed at the soldier. "He's fucken dead! He's fucken dead! What are ya doin?"

The driver, white as a cloud, was choking on fright. Louis was screaming and Jimmy yelled, "Go! Go! Go on, go!"

"Get off it! Get 'im out!" Louis hollered back.

Gunshots cracked over rooftops, then there was a crescendo of fire as the backup team and the Brits shot wildly at one another. Louis and Jimmy screamed at Higgins in unison,

"Go, go, go!"

That brought Louis to action, and he shoved the barrel of his rifle out the window. At the edge of his vision he could see Jimmy punching the dead man, shaking him and then punching him again. Buildings flew past as they raced up the incline of

Leeson Street.

"Fuck-all stop!" Louis yelled. The driver obeyed.

"Get him out!" Louis hollered.

Something had been released in Jimmy. He came back to the moment, understood, and shoved the crumpled man from the car. The driver roared off, fishtailing on corners, lips trembling to a mix of oaths and prayers, his features twisted in waxen fright. They skidded to a curb where teenage boys waited to take the guns and others stood with petrol. The trio jumped into the next car as the first erupted in snarling black smoke and the youngsters scattered with the rifles.

The IRA men raced on, dumping this second car and getting in another, and on to more snaking streets. Louis broke the silence.

"Jesus fucken' Christ!" He turned and looked at Jimmy, then swiveled forward. "Holy Mary mother of fucken' God!"

Now Higgins slowed, thinking, *nice and easy lad, don't need anyone's attention now.* Louis and the driver exchanged a look, then they watched the street. Higgins parked and the trio strolled down the sidewalk, down an alley, then to another and to the safe house.

Fetching a bottle of Jameson, the driver poured a shot, tossed it down, poured the other two a drink and another shot for himself. They fell onto a couch and two chairs, bonded forever, changed, reborn, scared shitless. Louis gulped the shot of whiskey and got himself another, Tommy Higgins held up his half-empty glass and got a filling squirt, Jimmy just sipped.

"What the bloody fuck-all was that?" demanded Louis.

"I thought we could take him hostage."

"Hostage! Hostage! He had more holes in him than a fucken' French whore house!"

Jimmy's only answer was to drain his glass.

"And what the hell were ye punchin' him for?"

A new shade of fear crossed Higgins's visage at the memory. He gaped at Jimmy who replied, "I was mad."

Louis turned to the driver. "Mad. He was fucken' mad. Out of 'is bloody mind."

For the first time Higgins spoke. "Near scared the piss out-a me. He's punchin' an' I'm near to pissin'."

The whiskey hugged and calmed them, drawing security around their hiding place. Jimmy felt the need to explain.

"He was a target of opportunity."

Louis seemed ready to answer but fell silent. Tommy Higgins was so exhausted he didn't think he could stand. The other two let Jimmy's words settle about the room. Legs were thrust out on the floor, chests caved in, their heads slightly back. Higgins spoke up.

"There's cards over by the lamp."

Louis glanced at the blue package of cards, then looked at Jimmy.

"Shit, if you'd brought yer fucken' friend we could play bridge."

They smiled, then shook their heads and howled with laughter. Gasping for air, they slapped their knees and held their stomachs. The shot glasses spilled their contents onto their hands and up their arms.

"He'd have the dead man's hand!" said Higgins.

"Aces an' fucken' eights!" shouted Louis.

They laughed until tears formed, and they laughed again. They laughed at the exhaustion that suddenly claimed them. All they cared about was that they were alive, that they could feel the sweet sweat pouring off each one of them, could smell the warm whiskey, could roll their heads back and murmur at the wonder of it all.

Jimmy had seen all of it as if floating above the ambush, like he was riding one of those big Hollywood cameras, swinging above the actors. That was how he had felt. He saw himself doing everything like he was watching a film. What would happen next? He'd had no idea. He'd never seen this movie before. He closed his eyes, surprised that he had no recollection of the dead soldier's face. He opened his eyes and the other two were staring at him. He waved the thick shot glass at them but didn't speak.

In the distance they could hear the whine of racing armored cars and the shouts of women, as British soldiers poured onto Catholic streets. Every bloke the soldiers sought was long gone, every woman and child they manhandled was fuel to a fire. A soft rain began to fall and British rage became confined to measuring tapes, geometry and the gentle rustle of reports insisting to be filed. In the little room the three men remained silent and the cards sat unturned, Jimmy glad for the latter, because he never could shuffle.

Louis Duffy, flat on the floor, tried to rise but the bodies atop him were too much. The three children squealed as their father struggled to get up, he made horse sounds and bear sounds, even announced he was a dinosaur, but still he was pinned.

"For God's sake you'll crush yer da, get off!" demanded Louis's wife, Marie.

The two boys, Brendan, four, and Thomas, six, were frozen by the order while their sister, seven, ignored it. But the pause gave Louis the opening he needed and he pivoted, spilling them all on the floor and attacked them with tickling fingers. Trapped, they howled for mercy as Marie put hands to hips and addressed her husband.

"Jesus, you're worse than they are!"

He looked at her with mock horror.

"Yer ma's needin' a good tickle!"

"Don't you dare!" Marie shouted. But the mob was after her and she ran to the kitchen where they got her, Louis lifting her from behind as she turned crimson with laughter and he let her down slowly then ordered the children to stop, which they did. Marie Duffy smoothed her skirt, cleared her throat and looked at all of them. "I'll get each of ya back in the bye and bye, so there's fair warnin'."

Louis looked at his kids. "Oh-oh. It was nice knowin' ya."

Laughing, they fled the room to sprawl on the rug in front of the television. The device, like every other television in Belfast was, day or night, simply, unfailingly, unquestionably on.

In the kitchen Marie turned back to the dishes as her husband came up behind her. He gently massaged her shoulders and she murmured softly. Then when she'd finished washing he put the plates away and with a hand to the small of her back they went to watch TV news. For two days the screen had been full of angry spokesmen decrying the depravity of the IRA. They accused the guerillas of repeatedly running over a wounded soldier then dragging him for blocks beneath the wheels of a car.

The whole area had lain low as enraged British Tommys had all but ransacked the neighborhood. Now the storm had slackened, and the routine of punch-counter-punch had returned. The Brits made an arrest and bottles rained down. The Brits fired rubber bullets, the kids threw rocks. One night a Brit patrol were certain they had an IRA man trapped in a dead-end alley. The soldiers fired down the alley, which turned out to be empty. As they pondered that mystery, a nail bomb arced over the buildings behind them. In the flash-bang silence that followed, a sergeant bellowed, "Damned Irish, they're like bloody rats!"

That became the catchphrase of the week, suitable for every occasion, especially when hollered at army patrols, in mock British accents, on the very darkest nights.

Louis Duffy checked the clock in the hall and announced it was bedtime. For once his brood went quietly up the stairs, and less then an hour later their parents followed.

Almost always sleep came quickly to Louis Duffy. He could snatch sleep in the smallest of spaces, he just thought of it and he was gone. But not tonight. His mind's eye wanted to show him memories and fears tonight. He saw himself and Jimmy stomping over the hills surrounding Belfast. Rousing field mice, catching glimpses of a rabbit they were determined to make a pet. Below them the city, its familiar pall of turf smoke snug over its gently terraced streets holding everything either of them had ever known. They stalked the rabbit most of that day but never did get him. The whole time Jimmy worrying about how they'd pay for his carrots and what to name him.

Eyes closed, Louis reached out to touch his wife's side. Reassured he took a deep breath and slowly let it out.

God, I never thought it would be like this. How will I survive the loneliness if they lock me up? How will I live without the touch of my wife and children? Dear God protect them. They say the Yanks sent their men to Vietnam for twelve months figuring a man can take anything for a year. What a luxury, he thought, being able to count the days down. And what is our measure? Standing up to them is all. Letting them know at long bloody last we are men and just as good as or better than them. All they had to do was admit that and go home. Just go home. There was the goal, there was the measure. Get off my street and go back to yours.

One of the boys muttered in his sleep and Louis tensed to the sound. Then he relaxed, the child was just dreaming, maybe not even that, maybe just talking in his sleep. Louis listened. All was quiet.

When it had all started, that had been the hardest thing to adjust to. They could kick in your door and do what they wanted to you. You were not even safe in your bed. That had thrown him more than anything. They could come right into your home for you. The police. It was the police who would break into your home in darkness. Not the criminals, the coppers. All here had learned to listen not for the burglar but for the law. *Their law,* he thought, *their law, my home.*

Now his mind showed him Jimmy punching the dead man. Punching, shaking him, the man's head flopping to one side, blood from both dead ears. Violating the dead. *God, is there any sin I'm not mixed up in?*

It will end one day. I can dodge them. No I can't. No one can. They will track us down one by one and others will take our place. They will track me down. They will pull me from this warm bed and kick me in the balls and throw me down the stairs and that will only be the beginning.

God, how deliberate they are when they beat you. So careful, step by step, like they're building something, something to be proud of. I went into that place in my soul and they couldn't get me. They couldn't get in. They couldn't break me. Told them a bunch of rubbish. Let them muck about the Falls Road and try to verify it. Jimmy too. Told 'em to fuck off.

Who do they think they are? Tromping all over the bloody world, walking on people. India, Pakistan, Cyprus, Aden, Palestine, Jordan. God, what people. The Yanks threw them out first and we'll be the last to get rid of them. What makes them think they're so damn superior? The instructors telling us their history, their arrogance and sense of entitlement. It's not personal they said. Not personal. It's the sweep of history, the struggle of the masses.

Tear down a street pissing your pants with your best friend in the back seat trying to kill a dead man. Then tell me it's not personal. This is the Falls. It's all personal. I hate the bastards. God forgive me, I hate each and every fucking one of them.

Sleep was closer, and he could see the grass of childhood he and Jimmy had walked upon as they trudged home.

"I was going to name him David," Jimmy had said of the rabbit. He'd stopped and looked mournfully at the wide fields leading to the hills, adding "now he doesn't have a name."

Louis had promised they'd return and capture David, but they never saw the white and brown animal again, and Jimmy never spoke of him, and Louis thought it best to remain silent too.

As he fell to sleep he dreamed of that time, the little boys, one grinning and holding the rabbit and the breezes brushing the hair on all of them. The boys walked down the hill, the rabbit peeking over Jimmy's shoulder at his wild home fading away, silently saying goodbye to the wind and rain, the fields and the fox.

In the small park the benches backed up to one another. The two men sitting there watched young women pushing prams, saw little boys running in chaotic patterns as the boys' sisters hopscotched in rhythmic delight. Ian MacDonald spread his right arm across the top of the bench and looked at the man near him who faced in the opposite direction.

"Who made the bomb?"

"I've no idea."

"Find out."

"I'll try."

"No, Jimmy, don't try. Find out."

The detective swept the area with a slow glance then spoke again.

"Who shot the two soldiers?"

The other man looked off before answering.

"Me an' Louis. We both done 'em."

The detective felt his anger swell at the answer. He had nearly exploded at Jimmy's earlier recitation of the ambush. His attacking the dead man and the chaos in the car before they threw the soldier out. Jimmy sensed the other man's ire. He turned and looked right at the detective.

"We was all shootin'. It was fuckin' chaotic. We was expectin that other jeep to roar back guns blazin'. Who shot them? We was both shootin, an' they was both shot dead. That's all I know."

Detective MacDonald turned away. He was momentarily distracted by the shouts of the children, but then he refocused.

Watching intently for a reaction, he asked,

"Have you heard anything about a sniper in the area?"

Jimmy seemed genuinely surprised.

"Not a word."

"Keep your ears open."

"I will."

The detective told Jimmy he wanted to go over everything again. From the beginning. Jimmy told him everything he could remember. Racing ahead, Jimmy would get caught up in the excitement of events, but the detective kept reeling him slowly back to examine every detail. As always Jimmy was impressed by this protestant thoroughness. He thought, *is that why they rule us? They build so carefully, they must think that way too. We're all shame and rage, songs and drink, we think everything's funny, while they plan and plan and only smile when they look down on us.*

"Any questions, Jimmy?"

He's getting nervous sitting here, thought Jimmy. It was true. Because one thing the lawman and the guerrilla shared was a dread of being seen together. Death had pulled up a chair at this meeting. And death would be present at every one of their rendezvous. And like a true whore, death would be happy to leave with either one, or both of them. Jimmy felt something press his side near his bottom rib.

"Take it," said the detective.

It was an envelope, and Jimmy shoved it into his coat pocket. He knew it contained pound notes. A single word pulsed brightly in Jimmy's mind. *Judas.* The words came out before Jimmy realized he'd spoken them. They were directed at no one.

"Now who am I?"

The detective's light brown brows went up in surprise. He leaned closer.

"Who are you? You're my enemy and I have sworn to defeat you." Detective MacDonald paused, the shouts of children pressing the silence between the two closer. "You're their enemy too. Oh, you're their very worst enemy."

Jimmy crushed the envelope in his pocket, squeezed it so tight it made sharp edges that bit into his hand.

"Ever seen a gyroscope, Jimmy?"

Jimmy's features relaxed, as if viewing an old familiar photograph.

"Aye. In school. Our teacher would balance it on the tip of a pencil."

Ian MacDonald nodded. "That's you. Balanced on the tip of that pencil. Enemies on all sides, enemies above and below." The detective adjusted his coat collar, then said, "Just don't become your own enemy. Remember that gyroscope. As long as it spins, it exists. I'm the string, I provide all the energy, you're that little gyroscope spinning happily. Got it?"

"I do."

The copper stood and looked down.

"A gyroscope, lad, a gyroscope. And Jimmy..."

"Aye?"

"Don't look down, it might stop your spinnin'."

At that point Jimmy felt his identity bleeding out of him, and wished the lads in balaclavas would emerge from the bushes to end it all. He would stand and face them. He would not whimper, not plead his case. He would stand like a man and embrace the bullets' peace. But only a little boy chasing a ball came close, and he looked at Jimmy and ran off tossing the ball in the air.

Jimmy waited and watched the cars go by and the children enmeshed in their games and circles. He glanced up at the few white clouds and at the playground, and realized here was a day when The Troubles were lying low. As he walked out of the playground and the two miles back to the Falls he realized that at least for today, with his crumpled pound notes, his shame and his wits, he could lie low with them.

Hide in plain sight. The sniper had always followed that advice, because he knew people see what they expect to see. A familiar scene will not elicit interest. He remembered a college lecture on social status and perception. Tell someone the man they're about to meet is a nobody and they'll say he's five-foot seven. Introduce the same man and tell them he's a PhD and an astronaut and he becomes six-feet tall. People see what they expect to see.

A little pile of dirt and broken pavement right next to a busy sidewalk would not be a place anyone would hide a sniper rifle. So early on a rainy night he had wrapped the weapon in plastic and put it there.

He had never tried to disguise the fact that he was an American. Rather, he'd made a point of announcing himself and playing into every TV cliché of what the Yanks were all about. Loud, throwing money around, and like the song said, *Don't know nothin' 'bout no middle ages, look at the pictures an' turn the pages. Don't know nothin' 'bout no rise an' fall, don't know nothin' 'bout 'nothin' at all.*

He greeted everybody and hugged them, he waved and said "How-do-you-do" to British soldiers, as the locals winced and shook their heads.

He bought rounds and marveled that they called potato chips 'crisps' and French fries 'chips.' He wished he could stay longer, he'd say, but he had to get back to school. Just came to trace the family and see the land. Such a pretty place, such lovely women and fine men. And, he didn't mind saying, he was scared silly. Nerves shot to hell and gone. How did they endure it? And, he would add, please come to America. Peace, love, get drunk, get tanned, easy money, take a break man.

Now he had this fine little nest. The place was full of them—empty houses, broken walls, debris fields, burned out cars and the skeletons of lorries. All set amid the smoky haze of peat burning sweetly and the incense-like memory of last night's arson. In the morning the sun rose and the buildings seemed stunned by what their windows reflected. It was Tet without the Viet Cong.

His journey took him to a tidy Dublin neighborhood with its doors painted in colors as extravagant as the residents were reticent. Then on to County Mayo. Or as the Irish called it, *Mayo God help us.* When Cromwell's Protestant army laid waste to Catholic land, some of the last resisters were shoved to Mayo. Hugging the west coast, sparse trees grown bent from Atlantic gales, its scattered population, mirror reflections of the trees, walking bent to history's winds, nailed to this reservation like red haired Indians. Saint Patrick fasted here on its highest peak, then descended to drive the snakes from Ireland. The snakes left behind their poverty, and Saint Patrick's heirs never could find the exit for that particular guest.

It was a brief meeting in a damp farmhouse. There were two of them. They were men of the land—tall, calloused hands, and lean, tough, suspicious, steady china blue eyes. Eyes he was to see here again and again. Eyes that laughed, blinked, then killed.

He told them the simple truth. He was a highly decorated combat veteran who looked like a high school teacher. He was now a college student and a crack shot. If they could provide him with the rifle he desired, he could raise holy hell for a month. Then he would be gone.

He did not tell them that when he'd come home from Vietnam he became a drunk, shooting out street lights in Boston neighborhoods. Or that, his war gone by, he fell into such a black depression he had to struggle to find the strength to dress himself, to shave, to open even one of the envelopes sprawled beneath his mail slot. Or that he hadn't been shattered by war, he had been shattered by the fat, smug self-assurance of his homeland living with eyes closed in its imagined peace.

He told the two Irishmen he knew they hated the Brits, but that he himself respected them. He knew history. Never underestimate the Brits. So he had one ironclad demand. Only the most senior people were to know he was there. Then leave him alone. Just tell him where the rifle was. He'd do the rest.

They left the room and spoke outside for ten minutes, then returned. Done deal. They shook hands and departed. Two days later a note was slipped under the door of his room in Dublin. The paper had a crude hand drawn map of the Falls Road with an arrow pointing to a house and the words, "under floor." In less than a week he was in that house holding the rifle.

The level of violence surprised him. It was much more intense and widespread than he had expected. Here the whole Catholic population was at war. Participation was the opposite of Vietnam. There the soldier started out at a base in the States as part of a great huffing and puffing war engine. That engine moved him steadily forward to combat, but at each stop in the inexorable journey, a piece of the machine, and its attendant people, fell away. The rear echelon types were spread across the Pacific, bellowing at you to hurry, irate at your stupidity, your confusion, as you stumbled forward while they stepped smartly back. Then when you finally got to the front, the loudmouths and kiss-asses were long gone, beside you was a muttering GI, and the only thing in front of you was your shirt.

That first day he was running late to find the little boarding house where the lady was expecting a student doing research. She had warned him it was a terrible time to be in Belfast. Terrible, terrible, terrible, she'd repeat every time he phoned. He moved quickly down the street and found the rooming house. Up five cement steps and that was that. He heard her footsteps on polished wood inside, saw her shadow through thin white curtains. *Knock knock. Who's there? Vietnam.*

Now nine days later he breathed in, then slowly out. He was fine. His heart rate was low, his palms dry. He'd found an old mattress in this abandoned house and set it against a wall nearby. It would help absorb the noise of the shot. He waited, he breathed and then the British soldiers came into view.

Again it was erotic, the sudden sexual rush stronger than ever, surprising him and scaring him enough to mutter "Christ" at whatever Freudian currents had been set flowing. These soldiers were more alert than the others. They moved very fast, pressing tightly to doorways, then sprinting, their rifles pivoting, always covering one another. But at this distance they might as well be unarmed.

He waited for the radioman, who would be near their leader. If he shot the radioman the leader might try to pull the wounded man to a safer place. That is exactly what happened, and he killed them both and he was gone.

That night he lay on his dark bed thinking of the fallen men. He recalled what Stonewall Jackson had told his Virginians when they shouted to spare a brave Yankee. "Shoot the brave ones and the cowards will run away."

He didn't believe there were cowards in the British Army. Just men like himself. Men who would not run but would momentarily freeze in place when chaos careened into their uniformed order. Thinking of it, he knew he could have shot two more of them. Why hadn't he? Was he a merciful killer, or afraid of getting caught? He forced those thoughts away.

"Don't think, do." He whispered, then repeated the words.

He pictured New England in autumn, saw himself walking down a lane of trees in morning light. He would do that when he got home, yes, and he would meet a wonderful woman and stop prowling the streets at night seeking peace in movement and blackness. His nightmares would leave him, he wouldn't need drink or dope, his rage would dissolve in sunshine. He could almost see it happening. Almost, but there was no color, like the view through the scope it was all black and white. He knew he needed that color back, knew it with all certainty, but even at sleep's precipice the colors shied from him.

The image of the girl behind the counter stayed with Jimmy as he walked. He imagined her hands squeezing his arm, they pressed close together, she putting her head snug against his left shoulder. Her image flicked away as he trotted across an intersection, but she happily rejoined him at the far curb. It was there he told her of her pretty smile, her lovely hair, how smitten he was at the instant of their encounter.

She laughed, giving him an affectionate tap on the arm, *Go on now with your flattery. It's true.* He breathed, almost aloud. *True*, he repeated inside his head. *The very second, that instant.*

He walked and their intimacy grew, their feelings like spreading roots in an underground embrace and she held him and understood.

How brave you are, she would say. *Brave, handsome and strong. No one could withstand that abuse. And still you carry on, still you have a plan to beat the enemy. Such a man you are, Jimmy. My brave, brave man.*

In the bustle of the pub, he could not hold onto her. Could not speak to the real girl in his imaginary world. Just next to his ear she whispered goodbye, giving a gentle kiss of understanding, *bye bye Jimmy, bye bye.*

Jimmy nodded to the bartender, who brought his pint. He gestured to the room's array of sipping men, as he sat at the bar with all the aplomb of a scarecrow. *Shoo birds, shoo, can't you see I'm a traitor?*

He drank, seeking messages in the rows of liquor above the bar, waiting for instructions from the bubbles zigzagging in the rounded glass. He peered closer, making sure there were no secrets lurking in the beer as he drained it, then ordered another.

Mellow now, he brought the girl forth. She sat close, taking his left arm in both of hers, pressing it to her, pressing as her head came to his shoulder, whispering for him alone. The others saw and the young were jealous, the old nodded in memory's fragrant groves, and his girl held him even closer.

Ian MacDonald's ugly face suddenly jumped out at him, barking once more. *Don't get drunk, Jimmy. People run their yap when they're drunk.*

He could handle another beer. He had a four-beer limit. He could handle three certainly.

The girl floated beside him again. She understood. A man takes a drink, sure every man does. She nodded, he winked at her, she smiled and Jimmy kept exploring the inviting faces of whiskey bottles for hints, allegations or clues.

The girl was right beside him. She was perfect in her adoration and understanding. He touched her arm, explaining he would be right back. He just had to sweep the room for the X on the treasure map, for the waters' fathoms and reefs, for the idol's stolen eye of erotic blue sapphire.

Michaela hummed through her chore of stacking cans on the shelf, thinking. *Lovely, he had lovely eyes and a fine smile. Eyes that held you while that smile touched you. A cute boy, lovely lovely boy. Lovely boy what's your name and where have you been?*

At Flaherty's Michaela worked the register, swept the floor, signed a receipt for a delivery of sugar, flour, baking soda and salt. Her fingers ran over the merchandise, her lips moving in silent cadence, counting, counting as the deliveryman watched her. *Oh yes he's a lovely boy, with soft blue boy smells and dreams, funny boy jokes and ways, naïve boy thoughts about perfumed downtown girls with hollow heels echoing on pavement.*

"One short on the salt," she said.

The man started, burly arms coming toward his chest, embarrassed at being caught in an error, more so at how quickly the woman had flipped the power fulcrum, one second avoiding his eyes, the next pushing him onto the defensive.

"Sorry," he muttered, blushing. He got another box of salt.

An honest mistake, thought Michaela, smiling to let the deliveryman off the hook. Smiling him out the door, smiling when he was gone.

Lovely boy come back, bring your bright eyes and smile, let me peer at them again and see what is inside.

Feeling like a man underwater, Jimmy approached the entrance to Flaherty's. Now his daydreams abandoned him, dropping their prepared scripts and scurrying for the shadows.

Inside the store he began a charade of awkward interest in things canned, wrapped and stamped.

Christ, she must think I'm an idiot.

Michaela had watched through the window as he approached, feigned indifference at his entrance, saw the reflection of the man in the little mirror over the counter. All the while she willed him toward her.

And he came. Bearing merchandise he didn't need, items seeming indignant at being used this way, things that squirmed from his grasp to slap the counter.

"Sorry," said Jimmy.

She didn't answer, only smiled, and he was lost, blushing and smiling back as she took hold of all that might be.

As he stepped back outside dreams bounced in line behind him, they were colors come to life, delighted to sing for their supper. He would return and ask her to accompany him. There was a dance in two days, he could do that, he could ask her there.

Her haughty dismissal, her mocking retorts, her public proclamation of his being a fool buzzed like mosquitoes about his head. He flailed at them as he walked back into the store. The part of the brown bag he gripped was damp as moss and he gave it a last twist as he approached her.

Her eyebrows were up, her head tilted back, her smile peeking out as he made his lips move and the smile broke free and she said yes.

Outside again the breeze applauded him, the dust rose in salute, and for this brief sojourn at least, a confident stride bore him forward. Inside, Michaela felt a warmth move against her. It touched her neck, her face and drifted off, promising to return and bring the lovely boy with it.

Liz Moran pressed both arms to her chest, the cigarette glowing harsh red in the cold breeze. Beside her on the fire escape Michaela had her own thoughts and her own cigarette. Liz spoke.

"So what's he like?"

"Who?"

Liz laughed aloud at her friend's attempt at nonchalance. She rapped Michaela on the arm.

"The one who put the sparkle back in your eye. Yer new man."

"He's not my new man!"

Another laugh, another rap.

"'Course he is! So what's he like?"

Michaela squinted at her trying to show a bit of annoyance but could not.

"He's sweet."

Liz waited, but Michaela closed her eyes and took a long drag on her cigarette. Exhaled.

"Christ, it's cold."

"If I want the weather report, I'll watch the telly. What's he like?" Liz teased.

Leaning back on the black metal railing, Michaela glanced off into the distance then refocused on her best friend.

"He's different. Like he's been really hurt inside. He's thoughtful of me, considerate."

"Do you think he loves you?"

That drew a dismissive sniff and another long draw from the cigarette.

"Do any of them love anything?"

Liz hesitated. She liked men, liked their walks and voices, their eyes and hair, loved their smells, the smooth muscles of them, the way they made her laugh, the way they made fun of one another's looks. She was never mad at men. Oh for sure, she'd had ones she could have throttled. But she was never angry at the whole bunch at once. Not the way Michaela could get. *Maybe*, she thought, *when you're smart, like Michaela, you get like that*. In school her friend was a wiz, even showing up the boys with the answers in mathematics. Then in the next class getting in trouble for correcting the teacher in history or grammar. Not in a polite way either.

Liz was burning with curiosity and sought neutral ground to draw her friend out.

"They're all so sweet when they're little boys."

Michaela gave a word in reply.

"Aye." She drew on the cigarette then spoke again. "I suppose he's quite taken with me. In that way they get when ya first know 'em." She dropped the cigarette and watched it tumble between the metal rails of the fire escape and plop on the pavement. "Does he love me? He could, I suppose. I loved him right off. Just like that. It was like he'd been there waiting for me all along and I just fell into it."

Liz was motionless, mouth slightly open, her cigarette's tip growing cold, sprouting a long gray ash. Michaela, folding both arms, looked at her and said,

"If you repeat one word, I'll kill you."

Jolted, Liz waved her arms.

"I won't, I won't, I swear! God strike me down if I speak!"

Michaela laughed and reached for her friend's arm.

"Let's get back to work, or we'll be hearin' old Flaherty's lamentin' about no good help an' how bloody impoverished he is."

Laughing, they slammed the door and went inside, where their boss was spluttering on the precipice of lecture, until Michaela silenced him with a look and greeted a customer.

The backroom ceremony needed no uniforms or medals, no speeches to underline its solemnity because its spectacle would vibrate outside on the street and among the people.

The local company commander, Mick Doherty, like many Falls Road men, worked in the city's slaughterhouses. Big Mick had a scar on his left cheek from his amateur boxing days, a scar on his right wrist from an English gunshot, and a presence that was itself as stark and powerful as a healed bullet wound.

Seemingly born to the cause, he referred to the three assembled guerillas as his cubs, and he kept them in line with a mother bear's simple instructions and coiled fury. In looks, words and deeds he fit the popular image of an IRA man. He did it without a thought, by his unwavering belief in the rightness of his cause, and by the simple formula of leading by example. Not a lot of people loved him, but every man he knew respected him.

He stood beside a representative of the guerillas' political party. Jim Noonan had, in the early days, picked up a gun but was far better with his gift of gab. He could, as the locals said, sell sand to the Arabs. He was the voice of reason, the face of regret and educated righteous indignation. He liked to tell the story of how the Brits beat the shit out of him at Hastings Street barracks, while their officer lectured him about an intelligent bloke like himself associating with IRA riff-raff.

Noonan had worn one of his suits today, the one with the vest, and he was a dapper exclamation point in a room of understated men. It was he who read the citation. The words came in and out of focus to the embarrassed young man in the center of the room.

"While on active duty . . . Volunteer James Michael Fitzgerald . . . complete disregard for personal safety . . . amid gunfire . . . seized a member of the occupying forces...though forced to release the occupier . . . gunfire . . . counterattack . . . the finest traditions of our struggle . . ." Then a dramatic pause, the paper now folded and by the reader's side, as he made eye contact with each and every man in the room and concluded, "Officer Commanding, Belfast Brigade, Provisional Wing, Irish Republican Army."

Then two solemn handshakes. Applause, afraid of itself lest it summon demons, more handshakes, Noonan's cologne wafting about. And it was over.

Neither Jimmy nor Louis spoke as they walked, hands thrust in pockets, down the incline of Leeson Street to the Long Bar. Louis paused at the entrance, held the door wide and spoke to Jimmy.

"Me thinkin' all along yer wires was crossed, but no, it was all part of a grand scheme. Citations from on high, right from the O.C., Belfast himself." Louis bowed deeply and gestured his friend to enter the pub, where they breathed in its beery welcome, nodded at friends and neighbors, then took a small round table.

Behind them the door opened again and Tommy Higgins entered. He stole a glance at Jimmy, a sideways look, as though seeking something he'd missed earlier. But accepting already the new version of things, ready to acknowledge to the chosen that yes he saw it, he was there, and that boy is bloody wired up, wired up, and fucken' fearless.

Their beers came in pint glasses, cool as October nights, and they sipped. It was delicious and they relaxed and leaned back in the chairs. Rewards were few in this business, and here was one of them. Praise from above, a reputation for their unit that would ripple through the city, and no pressure to carry out another operation. All that and blessed beer too. Tommy put out his hand to Jimmy.

"Congratulations. The Belfast O.C. himself."

Louis moved to break his friend's embarrassment.

"Ya know in France they'd have kissed ya on both cheeks."

"Ya can kiss me other cheeks," retorted Jimmy.

They laughed, they shifted their weight, they fell silent. The minutes passed and then Jimmy looked at both of them, put elbows on the table and leaned in to whisper, "So who the fuck's the marksman?"

His tablemates let their eyes wander the room and Louis replied, "Fuckin' Wyatt Earp. Yer man's dead-on. Four shots, four Brits dead. Some said from half-a-mile off."

Tommy added, "Aye. The radioman an' the officer. Bang, bang. Just like that. I heard the Brits never seen nothin', heard they was screamin' and cryin'."

Louis agreed. "Heard that meself. Heard the Brits never heard no shots, just saw the two go down. The whole bunch went over the edge, had to pack 'em off in Saracens so they did."

The men unconsciously looked down at the tabletop as though watching the scene play out. Jimmy interrupted their reverie.

"So who is he?" He knew he was pushing this subject, but knew he could get away with a gentle probe.

Tommy spoke.

"Heard he was from The Markets."

"That's more than I heard,' said Louis.

Tommy took that as a warning to shut up and he did.

"Markets?" asked Jimmy.

Tommy nodded his head *yes* but didn't speak.

Jimmy turned to Louis. "Ya think?"

Louis shook his head *no*. "I've heard nothin', Markets or otherwise. But I know if it keeps up, the fucken' Brits are comin' down on our heads. If he plugs another one around here they'll go bloody fucken' berserk."

Tommy Higgins took a long draught of beer and banged the glass down a little too loudly. "Kill twenty more, I don't care."

Louis shot him a look.

"You'll care when they're bouncing ya off the walls at Hastings Street Barracks." That silenced them all, and Louis immediately wished he hadn't said it. He added, "Fuck though. It's good to have some artillery on our side for once."

"Aye," said Tommy.

Louis nudged Tommy and gestured at Jimmy.

"Could be our friend here. He's full a' fucken' surprises."

They all laughed and Louis called for another round. Jimmy didn't speak until the beer came, scrutinizing the glass and seeming to address his words to it.

"Bloody strange, Wyatt Earp turns up in our midst and no one sees 'em ride into town is all I'm sayin'."

Tommy drew a breath to speak but a look from Louis silenced him. They let the words lie on the tabletop and they drank.

Louis looked up to see every man in the pub discreetly watching them. *Christ*, he thought, *they already know about Jimmy gettin' cited. They already know that and we don't know who's pluggin' Brits right down the street.* He wasn't aware of the smile that danced across his face as he thought *maybe we should just ask them. Jesus, maybe the wee ones in the park can tell us who the sniper is.*

More men entered the pub, most nodding to the seated trio, some nervously avoiding looking at them. As the place filled the three men finished their second beer and rose. They left by the back entrance as other men, done with work or another day on the dole, came in the front.

Lights out, the pale blue van coasted through the dark, the three men inside all leaning in different directions. Very good at his job, Davey Grant, the driver, slowly spun the wheel, easing into corners, anticipating the roads' bumps and wounds. He knew every one of these streets, had worked them for years delivering to the area pubs.

In the front passenger seat, Peter White remained stone silent as he always did when on a mission. He would not speak until they were out of this area, then he would take charge.

Behind them Monkey was crouched, his legs spread wide, both massive arms stretched out, grasping the canvas netting that ran along the roof. Monkey was beginning to get restless and could get out of control if something didn't happen soon. Monkey had a dock worker's bale hook on his belt, he had a straight razor in his dirty jeans, and he wore steel-toed boots. Unlike the other two he did not have a gun. Nobody was going to give a gun to Monkey.

The van glided down Leeson Street, the men inside eyeing the groups of youths on street corners.

"Too many," said Monkey.

They went on in the dark the driver at length answering, "Aye, too many."

On they floated in the smoky gloom, slowly, deliberately, into the wide waste ground off Grosvenor Avenue, left and left again back to the Lower Falls Road. The driver felt the gentle rocking as Monkey began to tug on the straps, and he exchanged a glance with Peter. Monkey broke into a sing-song chant, summoning his prey.

"Here Cat-lics, Cat-lics, Cat-lics. Here Cat-lics, Cat-lics, Cat-lics."

They swung back onto the wide expanse of Grosvenor Avenue. A half-mile away, Danny Hegarty, 17, cupped his hands to his face as he walked. His hands presented him the sweet perfume of his recently held love, Kathy Sweeney, 16. Danny planned to marry Kathy as soon as he could. He had a job, his parents loved Kathy, and her parents seemed to think the world of him.

Dropping his hands to his sides, Danny strode quickly along the uneven sidewalk. He went past the Grosvenor Arms pub, shuttered after a recent car bombing, and stepped onto the street to turn for his home.

Strong, young, energetic, with all thoughts to the future, he could not comprehend the sudden pressure squeezing his chest, preventing him from inhaling as his feet were lifted off the ground. *Something has me,* his mind hollered, *something has grabbed me from behind and it is carrying me!* The pressure squeezed him even harder as his strong arms grabbed at air, his feet flailed above the sidewalk and Monkey threw him into the open door of the van that rushed up out of the darkness.

There were no shots or screams, no roaring engine or squealing tires. The van slowly left the area, observing all rules of the road, and rolled toward the Protestant Shankill neighborhood.

Peter's turning in the seat and glaring was enough to keep Monkey in line during the ride, enough for him to temporarily control his sexual rages, his red screaming thoughts, his hook and straight razor. All that would come soon enough, and Monkey loved the hot yearning of the wait.

Slowly the van entered the car lot of a warehouse and Monkey carried their prize inside.

Two miles away Mary Hegarty wiped her hands on a dish

towel and stared at the clock. She went to the door of the small parlor where her husband was in his chair watching the late night news. She didn't speak to him but went back to the kitchen, annoyance and worry making a warm mix low in her chest.

She went to the front door, pushed it open and stepped into the gloom.

"He'll be along," her husband called.

Mary went back to the kitchen and took down some glasses from a shelf. She checked them for dust and decided to wash them all. When she had finished she was nearly frigid with dread.

The small parlor pressed close. So many blue eyes red with tears, black silence, hopeless gestures, such a stark and simple closed coffin. The old wept in free emotion, the middle-aged held one another's arms as they shuffled forward, faces tear-streaked, shaking their heads, holding the family, kissing them, while thinking *there are no words, no words.* Then the young people came, slapped by the sealed coffin, to never see him again, to never speak to him again. *His voice. Surely,* they thought, *we must hear his voice again.*

The neighbors kept coming, as outside on rooftops young men with rifles crouched low watching the street, wishing the butchers to dare come back now.

The IRA came, to offer condolences to the parents and to tell the men of the clan they would hunt down and kill the butchers. *We swear.* But no one was on the butchers' scent. People simply fell victim to them, and recently the kidnappings had been moving steadily closer, until young Danny had been snatched right at the end of the street. The people had grown used to the bombings, the shootings, the army raids and the beatings. But here a trap door had opened to bottomless black space and the damp darkness from below touched where they stood to chill everything inside them.

The next day when Michaela arrived at work Liz Moran grabbed her arm and hurried her to a doorway. Liz was shaking as she spoke.

"I heard it was vampires. There's vampires about."

Her first impulse was to be sarcastic, but Michaela could

see her friend was terrified. She put her hand on Liz's shoulder.

"It's awful, so it is. But it's only men doin' it."

Liz didn't hear.

"They follow the scent of evil. If there's enough evil, it draws 'em so it does."

Liz grabbed Michaela's arm, digging her nails into the skin.

"I didn't sleep a wink last night! I'm only goin' out in daylight! They're here, they're prowlin' the night!"

The other woman's terror crackled to Michaela.

"Jesus Liz, stop it, there's no such thing."

Liz put her cigarette to her lips, shaking her head yes.

"I heard they come with the German bombers in the war. They fell out of the sky with the bombs and lay asleep 'til now. We made 'em come back to life! It's all the bad things that's been done here! We all done it, we brought 'em!"

The boss came to the front of the shop, looked down at them and pointed to his watch.

Michaela took both the other woman's hands in hers.

"We'll talk later, I promise."

"Jesus, I'm scared."

Michaela gave the hands a gentle shake.

"We'll talk. It will be alright."

Watching her friend walk hurriedly to her work station, Michaela knew it would not be alright. She'd closed her ears to descriptions of what had been done to the boy. She told the speakers to be quiet, to change the subject, but they would not, they could not. At one point she'd pressed both her hands to her ears and walked away.

Dear God, save us. Who could do such things? They're here. They're here and we pass them by and don't know, then at night they turn into beasts and hunt us down. She shivered and went for her sweater which rested on a stool nearby

What must the Butchers look like? They can't look normal, there must be some sign, some kind of mark to them. Vampires, Je-

MOLLOY

sus. Vampires falling from the night sky, falling from Nazi planes.
She shoved her thoughts behind a door, the door slid open and then she slammed it shut.

In a few moments she looked at the first customer of the day and asked how she could help her.

The two men walked rapidly away from each other, neither turning to look back, though each had the other's image burned in his brain, could see the other striding off across imagination's landscape.

Detective Ian MacDonald was hot with anticipation, hurrying forward to the details, to overcoming the bureaucratic objections, setting in motion the plan, the men, the trap. Jimmy staggered beneath his emotional load, closed his eyes to dizziness and kept walking, the crumpled cash in his pocket shouting out what he had done. Again.

At the beginning he had thought *surely there will be a bottom to this dread of myself.* But there was no nadir, no soft muddy floor to this pond from which to push back to the surface. There was just the dried mud from before, and the sinking wet muck of the now. And the emptiness within seeking to suck dry his skin and bone.

Summoned, he had decided to resist. And the copper had plucked his resistance clean with a few words, a look, a poke of an index finger.

The copper knew some things, and when they parted he knew all the things about the upcoming operation. The time, the participants, the bomb, the cars, the routes, the safe house. Just like that.

The copper said *Make an excuse at the safe house. Tell them you have to make a phone call, you need some fresh air, you saw something suspicious outside, say anything, just don't be in the house. When you leave we will see you. We'll search the whole neighborhood and make it look like we stumbled upon them. Then we'll arrest them and no one will get hurt. On either side.*

Jimmy had muttered his acquiescence but he could not picture Big Mick being taken by a shouted command from an Englishman. That Irishman's hatred of the Brits was learned at his father's knee, it was his family inheritance, his sacred vocation.

As he walked, Jimmy forced his mind to settle upon the operation to bomb Agnew's Department Store on the Protestant Shankill Road. Two-hundred pounds of gelignite in the bomb car. A driver and passenger in that vehicle, two men in the getaway car behind. As soon as the bomb vehicle was parked in front of the store there would be a phoned warning giving the police a code word and 20 minutes to clear the area.

They had all done this before, which guaranteed nothing. There were so many factors in play on the streets of Belfast that anything could happen. Here experience only meant knowing that you had cheated death before. And dreading the little white ball bouncing on the roulette wheel, because that little white ball was you.

But Jimmy's whispered words on a park bench ensured that no one would go on this particular tense drive to a proud Protestant enclave. Because Belfast's herd of stampeding furies had turned into a wide noose with its center at the house where Jimmy's best friends would gather.

The woman considered the unlit cigarette in her hand then looked across the roof at the man who faced away from her.

"Tell me about your loves, Jimmy Fitzgerald." Michaela saw the shoulders of the man tense, as though he'd been unexpectedly poked from behind. He didn't turn but stayed motionless, staring at the setting sun as it inhaled the peat smoke of a thousand little houses.

When Jimmy did turn, the sunset was a watery pastel in his eyes, his features soft in the falling light.

"Me an' love is a short tale."

She lit the cigarette, lips tight on the butt, then flicked away the match. She spoke with the cigarette on her lips.

"No joking, tell me."

He knew she was dead serious. He told her of his first kiss, an awkward soft colliding of faces in the shelter of a doorway with the rain cascading down three feet away. And the girl running off into the downpour never to speak to him again. And girls at dances with warm mouths and breasts locked away beneath inscrutable feminine attire. And later, girls at parties, shockingly willing and afterwards perfectly uncaring. He stopped talking.

She made him start again by saying, "And?"

He turned his palms outward closing his eyes to memory.

"There was a girl once, when I was sixteen. She was seventeen. Her name was Anna Marie. My da knew her da. They lived in Turf Lodge."

He stopped, as far off dogs barked, startled from their routine, something that could only mean trouble. But the animals fell silent and he continued.

"She had big brown eyes and long straight brown hair. I took her to the cinema once, back before all this fightin'. When ya could go about town like. We never more than held hands, but I loved her so." He stopped. He could almost feel her hand pressing his.

"Ya know, the way kids do. I think she felt the same. Then her family moved away. Just like that. Across the ocean to Canada to one a' them provinces they got way in the west of Canada. 'Course she knew they were goin', but she never told me. Not 'til they were packin' up to go." The sun was half buried in the hillside, and he added, "She had tears in her eyes. An' we didn't even hug goodbye. Then they were gone an' I never heard from her, not ever."

Against the sun Michaela was a small silhouette and he said to that black shadow,

"That's the story of me an' love."

Far down the street a mother called her children to supper as Michaela moved to embrace the man. She put both arms around his neck and pulled him close to kiss his lips. Then she held his face in both hands to whisper, "I'll not be goin' away."

They stood in embrace until they stood in darkness and they didn't say another word. Even when they went back inside they didn't speak, then on the sidewalk they held hands and walked. Several times they paused in doorways to kiss and smile and tell one another of their love. They parted at her door and she went inside her small flat, where she tidied up the rooms.

Jimmy Fitzgerald was in her heart now, had entered on the strength of his honesty, his openness, the pain he'd known, his courage, his shy smile, the way he held her hand as they walked. Michaela could see them together, could see where the furniture would be, what meals she would prepare, who would visit, and she could see children.

She could not see peace. Not yet. She had given up guessing when the fighting would stop. Now however she had carved a small place of rest within this violent world. A small place where there would be Jimmy and children, friends and family. She could see that small place, a haven from the outside, a raft they could float upon until the world outside regained its sanity. She could see all that very clearly as she let herself sink into loving, then into sleep.

Blocks away Jimmy stood and watched his parade of secrets stomp past and when all the hidden had gone by, he stood listening to the fading echoes of his shrouded marchers. If he told her everything she would be party to betrayal. He would paint her the wrong color in a black and white world.

If he told her nothing she would be partly protected. Safe until MacDonald decided she too could be used. Or until the copper slipped word to the IRA she was part of Jimmy's betrayal.

Jimmy decided to focus only on his relationship with this woman. When the time was right they would flee. To America, to Australia, to that part of Canada where the prairie rolled to the horizon.

He would keep her safe and they would start a new life. When he was ready. When the copper's guard was down. She'd understand and go with him. Until then he would hold his secret close, a thing apart from his feelings for her. A man could do that, a man had to play the cards he was dealt.

He walked down the street to the Grosvenor Road where evil came on four wheels, and he didn't care. He wasn't afraid of them because he almost knew who he was now, could almost see the way ahead and to hell with them all.

It was that part of the operation when you sit still and silent, time piling up around you, slowly pushing you into what filled the air of the room and what waited ahead and you try not to shake, try to keep your voice from wavering. Because death is outside tapping its foot, for it is on a schedule, your schedule, and you can't be late, so you sit and feel the sweat on your skin and heated sticky dread kicking your stomach from the inside.

The four of them—Big Mick, Tommy, Louis and Jimmy—sat quietly because that was one of Big Mick's rules.

"No joking," he ordered, "it's not a damn show on the telly. Check your weapon once and put it down, there won't be an accident if nobody's fiddlin' with a bloody Armalite. Go over what you're to do in your mind, then when we're ready, you'll be ready."

Tommy, who again would be driving, sat with his hands folded, eyes closed, fingers nervously maneuvering the streets he had memorized. Big Mick was impatient, longing to close with the enemy, to knock down one more of their damned buildings, to extinguish another tiny piece of the English embers that lay all over his being.

Louis sat next to him, going over old films he had seen. Trying to remember the names of all the characters and the actors who had portrayed them. He was right now stuck on the name of the fellow who played Doctor Watson in the old Sherlock Holmes films. Damn, what was his name?

Jimmy was opposite all of them, wishing everything away,

thinking of his excuse that he felt ill and needed medicine. When he spoke there was no need for acting because he did feel sick, and he got permission to run up the street to the chemist.

"I'll go with ya," said Louis, and he got a nod of approval from Big Mick.

He's coming, Jimmy thought but could not come up with more than that. *He's coming with me.*

"Hurry up," was all the Big Mick said.

The outside air was cold, focused in the narrow lanes that squeezed it, hurried it along as it hit the two men, bending them forward.

"Alright?" asked Louis.

"Me stomach's upside down," said Jimmy.

Louis grunted his sympathy as they walked across the road and entered O'Connor's chemist shop, its little bell arched above the door announcing them. Louis grabbed a fistful of chewing gum, mints, and several peppermint candies all new in their twisted cellophane. Jimmy lingered over a row of medicines, unable to focus, sweat beaded on his forehead.

William T. O'Connor, 44, bald and boring as was his father and grandfather before him watched his customers. If this man had an opinion on anything other than the weather, no one had ever heard it, and if he had an opinion now it was invisible.

"May I help you, sir?"

Louis answered for his friend.

"His stomach's gone sour. Turned over, upside down it is. Can we right it?"

O'Connor gently, briefly, closed his eyes at this mocking of the wonderful complexity of human digestion and said,

"Top shelf, right in front of you, sir. Coats the lining, should do the trick."

Louis plucked the package from the shelf and went to the register saying,

"This round's on me."

"Anything," said the shopkeeper, not reaching the next word, interrupted by the sight of British troopers pouring past on both sides of the street and the roaring of armored cars as they thundered from every direction. O'Connor never changed expression as Louis spun around, turning chalk white.

"Fuck all!" he cried, and Jimmy realized he had not thought past this point and he froze.

Louis grabbed his friend's arm, throwing the candy on the counter.

"C'mon." he whispered. Then he punched the air in the direction of the chemist.

"We weren't here."

The two ran around the counter and out a back door. There was a low fence, a yard, another low fence and an alley beyond.

Far off an English voice bellowed, and was greeted by the rapid barking of an Armalite. Over the roof there were men's screams, a nail bomb, another and another and an answering crescendo of English fury.

Using houses as shortcuts the two men ran into a neighborhood that seemed to suddenly tilt on its side with its contents spilling over them. They bounced off front doors, televisions, women, chairs and tables. Faces leaped at them—housewives, children and fathers, a freeze-frame of shock, as Louis and Jimmy kept pounding through dwellings. They ran outside, inside through a home and out onto the next street, thudding through more homes, more stunned faces, out, in, running, running, banging into doors, on and on, until they were blocks away and inside with fingers to lips shushing a family of four. A family that could only gape at what had crashed upon them, as surprised as if the sea had tossed these two apparitions into their parlor. In their wake doors were locked and families mute, no one had seen anything, and the British soldiers were piling up in frustration kicking locked doors and locked lips.

Even from here Louis and Jimmy could hear it, another ripping of air as a nail bomb went off, but no more of the Armalite's call, just the steady, murderous roar of the British SLR rifles.

The two gasped, unaware of their cut clothing, their bleeding scrapes as the family stared at them, fascinated by the little pink bottle Jimmy clutched.

"What street is this?" Louis gasped.

"Stafford," said the housewife.

"Stafford," repeated Louis.

Jimmy nodded that it would be a good place.

"We'll stay 'til it's dark," Louis told the family.

They said they understood, and the two comrades went upstairs and sprawled in a small hallway. Later the woman brought them tea and cake and they thanked her. They didn't speak, for there was nothing to declare. There was only the question of whether the men they loved were alive or dead.

In two hours the telly told them the awful final truth. Then, still crouched on the floor they put faces to the crook of their arms and sobbed into merciful sleep.

Soldiers stood on rooftops, in windows, at every curb and street corner. Soldiers draped like green bunting upon their armored cars, soldiers squinted into telephoto lenses. Still other soldiers crowded them as they bore upon their shoulders the coffins of Big Mick and Tommy Higgins. The British were an armed wall all around, saying *look at us, our numbers, our skills, our machines, our technology. We are stronger than you.*

The Irish, unarmed, silent, footfalls in slow cadence carrying their martyred dead, basking in their ancient rituals, replying. *Look at us, we are better than you.*

As the British gripped their weapons the IRA began to materialize in front of them. Men in masks, women and children crowding close. Now the honor guard, green jackets, black berets, masks, to place a black beret and pair of gloves upon each coffin. At a low command, the coffins hoisted to the guards' shoulders. Now forward toward the end of the block where the hearse waited.

The soldiers leaned in to brush against their enemies, to not yield one inch of this place. The mourners pushed slowly through, the families squeezed tight, the parents, the widows, the brothers and sisters, the children, shoving against the strong arms of the British, pushing forward.

The British allowed them through, squeezing them, smirking, looking down from rooftops, staring and staring at them, as near the hearse the crowd grew to thousands, and more thousands moved toward it and waited along the route to the cemetery.

On the route the soldiers were gathered in large groups at key intersections, green knots to the flowing ribbons of Irish mourners who lined the sidewalks.

At the cemetery Jimmy and Louis stepped forward, the black mask sucking at the tears that fell freely from Louis's eyes. When they lifted the coffin to their shoulders, Jimmy felt the furious eyes of the dead upon him, heard them whisper at him to keep away.

Step left, again, and thrice more, turn slowly, and from the coffin a whiff of the destination awaiting them all. Halt. Turn again. From the crowd masked men with pistols suddenly appeared, raising the guns in salute. One, two, three volleys.

Jimmy stood straight, the back of his knees aching, his throat dry as words sprinkled on him and fell on the grass nearby. Words of anger, grief, hope, indignation. Words of prayer.

Pray, he told himself, *pray for the dead*. He tried. He could not bring his thoughts into focus. *Pray*, he told himself, but all he could do was endure the two gaping holes in the soft earth, the sobs of the women, the coolness of the soldiers in the distance watching and watching, and the radiating heat of his race's rage.

On command he snapped to attention and executed his salute, closing together heels, his left thumb perfectly on the seam of his trousers. The bugle played, their flag of rebellion was folded, the beret and gloves presented and wrung dry by the widows.

The hard men melted away, the guards of honor faded into the crowd that began to dissolve.

In an uneven circle all around the soldiers watched, thinking, *if we peer close enough we will see the marrow, the mind, the reason why. We will glean their secret and use it against them.* In crisp military discipline they kept staring, until the thousands had dispersed and all they could see were Catholic workmen with shovels for their task, and red bandanas for their sweat.

Louis pulled up tight to the bar, one hand holding the pint glass, his shoulders hunched forward, as though braced for a sudden gale. He was storm-blown, bruised inside and out. He kept a palm at the edge of the bar, as if expecting the place might give way beneath his feet.

Upended by the utter indifference of God, Louis had sunk into himself, into a mind like an alarm gone mad, throwing off fears with no way to silence the clanging bell. The dance of these formless dangers paralyzed the man watching them. He should be doing something, planning, moving, but had no idea what or how. He had always moved with the squad. Now half the squad was dead, and though he could not have formed the words, he knew in his heart the other survivor was far more damaged than himself. His thoughts were like a record that kept skipping, to play the same notes over and over.

Did they stumble upon us, or were we betrayed? Did they get information from Big Mick and Tommy before they died? Were they just now pulling at the thread that would lead to me? To Jimmy? Poor Jimmy, throwing up and throwing up in the hallway. Thank God the man was taken ill, and thank God I decided to tag along. For a pack of gum. Christ, I'm alive because of a pack of gum.

He still had the gum in his pocket, now too superstitious to chew it or throw it away. The weight he'd lost in the last few days was obvious, as his clothes hung loose. There was a layer of heat between his flesh and the clothes, and he took his coat by the lapel and shook it. He could feel the heat rise and dissipate, letting him know how vulnerable he was.

The door swung open, sunlight stabbing across the floor. A shadow flashed, then the door swung shut. He shouldn't be here. A pub was the first place they'd look, that was basic. But right now the basic was too complex for him and he took another hard slug of the beer. Christ, he thought, *it's the only thing holding me together.*

"How ya doing?"

Louis started. The Yank was looming over him. Christ he was tall. One of us but stretched out. He moved in a different way. That walk, like a cowboy, slow and sure.

"Sorry, didn't mean to startle you."

"That's alright, Yank. How ya getting' on?"

The man slid onto a stool, leaving an empty seat between them.

"Pretty good, no complaints. You?"

Louis's glance met the barman's and he almost smiled. The Yank missed the slight mocking of his vernacular.

"Pretty good, mate, pretty good."

The barman knew the American's preference and brought a beer and a shot of whiskey.

"Another one?" asked the American, pointing at Louis's glass. "It's on me."

Louis managed to almost smile.

"That being the case, I will have another."

The American sipped his beer and sniffed the whiskey, speaking to the shot glass.

"Those funerals were something. I never saw anything like that before."

"Aye, somethin' alright," said Louis.

Taking another sip of beer the American peered at the shot glass, as if he'd dropped something precious into it. He spoke to his own reflection in the mirror.

"Those goddamn Brits. One of 'em shoved me as I walked

past him. Bastard almost knocked me over."

Louis smiled at the barman, then turned to the Yank.

"They enjoy throwin' their weight around alright."

"Tough guys," the American said sarcastically to the mirror. "Too tough for 'Nam."

With that he raised the shot glass and swallowed its contents in one gulp, exhaling as he gently rapped his chest with curled fingers.

"You in Vietnam, then?"

The man started, a redness spreading on both sides of his neck.

"No, no I wasn't. I'm a teacher. Never served."

Louis nodded his understanding and watched the Yank's reflection in the mirror.

He's lying.

Louis understood that the man's mask had slipped. It slipped to reveal the bitter contempt for the Brits who didn't help their friends fight in the jungle. It had popped out, and he had shoved it back inside. Louis didn't try to get at any truth, but he filed the feeling away. The Yank was in Vietnam and he's concealing that fact. Why would he do that, and why was he here? Louis sat up straight. He could hold on to this puzzle, he could focus on it, it could help him remember who he was.

"So what do ya think a' this place then?"

The big man shifted, sipped his beer and turned, his left elbow on the bar.

"Man, before I got here I thought there'd be kids throwing rocks, an occasional car bomb somewhere. I never thought it would be this intense. No shit, you got yourself a full-blown conflict here. I mean flat out urban warfare. It ain't getting reported back home." He gulped half his beer, spreading his arms out to address the barman. "Jesus, Peter, what was it Friday, two dozen bombings?"

"Twenty-four on the nose, Yank. Two dozen separate car

bombs."

The American let loose a low whistle, asking rhetorically, "How do they do it? There're Brits on every street corner downtown. How the hell do they do it?" He drained the remnants of his glass saying, "I don't know who they are and I don't want to know. But those IRA boys got brass balls. Brass fucking balls."

The door swung wide as three young men from the neighborhood came in, laughing at something that had been said outside. The American stood as the newcomers crowded the bar calling to the barman.

"Gotta go. Good talking to ya."

"Cheerio, Yank," said Louis.

Louis watched the window, saw the Yank's shadow flit by, then turned to the task of drinking. Peter came and scooped up a handful of coins the American had left, then announced,

"Some people still know how to tip."

"Peter's made his day's quota then. We're off the hook," one of the young men said to the room. The young men laughed and Louis smiled as Peter went to the back room to get more bottles, more glasses, and to roll out a keg of Guinness.

The raucous trio moved to the dart board as Peter returned to stand near Louis who asked,

"So who's our friend?"

Peter shrugged.

"Comes in every day, has a pint and a shot and leaves. Says he's researching his ancestors. Goin' home in two weeks. Pleasant fella, well educated, from Boston."

"And a good tipper," said Louis.

"Well I didn't want to press the point. But if all the customers was like him I'd be drivin' a Jaguar."

"He's a school teacher?"

"That's what he tells me."

"Not too fond a' the Brits, is he?"

"That's the first time I heard him even mention 'em."

Two more men entered the pub and Peter went to them, leaving Louis to say to himself, *none too fond at all.*

The Yank popping up in their midst brought other things into focus for Louis, opening an intravenous drip of energy that allowed him to push away his empty glass and stand.

"I'm away then, Peter."

"Cheerio, Louis, watch yourself."

Tight against the pub's wall, Louis let the raid run again in his mind. The force that arrived, the way they deployed, their volume of fire.

"They knew," Louis whispered to no one.

His da had always told him to never accuse a man of a thing unless he'd seen the transgression with his own eyes. He had not seen the act, but had barely survived its consequences. Something was moving offstage, but Louis was not one to tackle a blowing curtain.

The sniper was shaken. He had stumbled and that Irish guy had seen it. Louis, that was his name, Louis. Bastards were sharp as tacks. No education, dressed like hobos, no jobs, but they sat around reading Plato, Tolstoy and Freud.

Telling himself to be calm, he recognized the jitters pulsating within, because he had had them before. He was going home soon. He was a short timer. They used to joke at base camps, "I'm so short I gotta look up to tie my shoes." Guys would make that joke and then they were gone. Not home gone. Dead gone.

Fate loved to play with soldiers. And all the poor soldiers had to fight back with were good luck charms and stenciled phrases on helmets. It was mojo versus the beast, and the beast would not be denied. Short-timers just seemed to get killed. Everyone knew it. It was too scary to study, too close to touch. It was just what it was. So he had never counted days aloud as it came time to leave that place. Not once. And he'd made it. He would make it again.

Back home he hadn't been able to let it go, he kept seeing the faces, kept hearing the voices shouting in their native tongues. But he didn't do so in melancholy horror, but in distant longing. He'd found his country ready to declare all its returning warriors to be damaged goods. A nation that would sigh and whisper and want them to just go away. And soon they came to think of themselves that way too. And like the others he played the role that had been assigned to him.

Almost. Because though he never put it in so many words, slowly he came to realize his life had been the wound, green-leafed firefights the balm.

Now his mind kept rushing him back to childhood. He could hear those days, could feel the saliva spray bounce off the bully's thick lips with punches, feel the laughter of the cool kids, the sarcasm of the teachers. It kept coming back, louder and sharper. Not Vietnam but childhood, middle school, high school teachers, giggling girls. It was getting too loud, too sharp. He couldn't turn it off.

He needed another drink. Down the Falls Road was another pub, with one plate glass window freshly boarded up, the other one time-stained and breaking sunlight into streaks as he stepped inside. Several men at the bar turned, with the collective slow movement of the predator. The men were heavy set, grim, with caps low over their eyes, and being perfectly of this time and this place they exuded a force that made him fidget for his wallet. They stared for long seconds, appraising, then turned to discreetly watch him in the mirror behind the bar. He ordered his beer and a whiskey chaser, the room relaxing a notch at his accent, the men resuming their muffled conversation.

He suddenly remembered once being warned not to go to this bar. Hard men, they told him. The hard men drank there. He had been told similar things about bars in the States. But there was an unspoken rule in these places. You could come in and have your drink and leave. Just don't come back, don't think you belong. You don't. You are not one of us and never will be. He never tried to be one of them, so he had always been able to move among them. Briefly.

He gulped the whiskey and told the barman the truth.

"I needed that."

The man smiled.

"Another, then?"

"No, all set, thanks."

He sipped the beer, watching the street. He was tipsy. The

beer and chaser would make him more so. He decided not to say anything more, would let them reach their own conclusion. That in a city of sudden blind violence, something had scared the hell out of this Yank. The man had needed a stiff drink and taken it. They could understand that.

He finished the beer, thanked the barman and left. He didn't look to see if other eyes followed his exit. He didn't have to. He could feel their heat burning right through the back of his shirt.

Ian MacDonald eased off the gas pedal, his gaze drifting left and right as he cruised past his street. There were no pedestrians, no strange vehicles. He again checked the rear view mirror. He was not being followed. Nevertheless, he drove on, going south five minutes then reversing course to come at his home from another direction. There had been no security alerts, which meant it was more tempting to fall into a routine. And routine could be fatal. Routine was his enemy, and his enemy's friend.

He stopped in front of his house, one hand on his holster, the other touching the keys in the ignition. He shut the car off.

Lauren pulled the door open and locked it tight behind him, and the love of his woman and his child pressed him, revived him and let him exhale.

"How's my wee man, then?" asked the detective.

"Excellent, Daddy. Daddy, there are nine planets. Nine! Did you know that?"

The detective exchanged a smile with his wife before replying, "Nine! That's quite a crowd. And where are these planets?"

"In space, Daddy."

Ian MacDonald slipped his hand onto the boy's shoulder, guiding him toward the living room saying, "Well, let's hear about these nine planets in space."

His wife brought his drink.

"And how was Mummy's day?"

"Mummy's had a lovely day."

"Daddy's day was manageable, and that's OK with Daddy."

The boy slipped beneath his father's left arm, pressing close to the reassuring warmth and bulk of the man. Ian MacDonald listened patiently to facts about Mars and Venus, and the amazing heat of Mercury. Lauren MacDonald interrupted to announce their supper was ready.

They were almost finished with the meal when the phone rang. Lauren answered it, listened for a few seconds, and when her features fell, he knew the call was for him and that it was bad news.

"Detective Sergeant MacDonald?"

He recognized the voice of Captain Frost, the liaison between the army and Special Branch.

"Speaking."

"There's been a shooting, Sir. Multiple casualties, in the Lower Falls, Sir."

The detective wrote down the directions, told his wife he was sorry, kissed her and the boy goodbye, and went to the door. The sun was lowering, all looked clear, and he departed for Castlereagh station, where an armored car would bring him to the location of the shootings.

He arrived at a scene that looked like a violent storm's aftermath, debris scattered, victims stunned and repeating to one another what had occurred. The storm's fury had focused upon a Saracen armored car, both its rear doors open wide, its green snout slammed against a house. Like white envelopes carrying condolences, shards of the house's masonry were sprinkled on the Saracen's hood.

The young detective on scene was obviously relieved to see him. All around them British soldiers were running, dragging civilian males into armored cars, shouting, swearing, pointing, warning and threatening.

Even as the detective took this in a company of paratroopers arrived, distinct in their maroon berets as they sprinted down streets and alleys. Civilian men cringed at the sight of the dreaded Paras, women clutched their hands to their throats, lips moving in silent prayer. These were the shock troops of Belfast. Tough men, angry, skilled and determined, and among Catholics they had a fearsome reputation for brutality.

Detective MacDonald pushed all that out of his mind and focused on the young detective whose name he had heard a dozen times but could not recall.

"Tell me what happened. Start at the beginning, go slowly and don't leave anything out." *Bell, that was his name*, remembered Detective MacDonald. *His name is Brandon Bell.*

"Yes, Sir. The army squad was in that Saracen." He turned and gestured. "Something caught their eye and they stopped. When the sergeant opened the rear door he was immediately shot. He fell to the street. We think the same shot hit the driver in the back of the head, because at the first shot the Saracen lurched into the house. There were three more shots, straight into the open rear door. So five men were shot. Four are dead, Sir. One had a bullet through his arm. In one side out the other. He got it when he reached out to slam the door shut. Probably saved more from getting killed. He'll recover."

Detective MacDonald nodded.

"I'll speak to him as soon as it's possible."

"Yes, Sir."

"Anything else?"

"There's one squaddie unscathed. I spoke to him. Not much help there I'm afraid."

"Other witnesses?"

"The usual, Sir. No one knows anything."

MacDonald grunted. "We'll see about that."

They both looked around, then both instinctively looked in the direction opposite the armored car's open rear doors. The direction from which the shots came. MacDonald turned back to the Saracen.

"Let's have a look, then."

"Yes, Sir. Pretty grim inside, Sir."

Without replying Detective MacDonald strode to the armored car, nodding respectfully to the nearby soldiers, bracing for what he would see. What he saw were hastily ripped and bloody compresses, discarded syringes, shreds of fatigues cut off by medics, and on the front seat a piece of skull, blonde hair attached. And blood. It was everywhere. On the floor, the two parallel benches, the ceiling. He hesitated. The blood on the floor, coagulated now to a near-brown porridge, must have been an inch deep. He had no choice. He stepped carefully inside for a closer look.

The detective noted with professional detachment that a bloody imprint near the driver's view slit matched the contours of the section of skull. He imagined the scene.

The sergeant opens the rear door and they all prepare to scamper out. *Bang!* The sergeant falls and the driver's head explodes. The vehicle lurches and slams into the house. Before they can react—*Bang!*—another one is hit. There must have been panic. Get out or stay in? Their training said *jump out*. But what would they be jumping into? Then *Bang!*—another one slumps dead. Pandemonium in their cramped metal world. Then *Bang!*—another one hit. One collects his wits enough to reach out and slam the door, and pays for it with a high powered bullet through his arm.

"Jesus," he said, as he stepped back out.

His own family flashed before his mind's eye. He'd just held them hadn't he? It seemed unreal now. For that matter, what lay before him also seemed unreal. He turned to the young detective and gave a rare compliment.

"You've done a good job here. But I'm afraid if we're going to find out anything it will be from a witness."

"Yes, Sir. Thank you, Sir."

The far off screams of women came over the roofs. The

sound was the cry of a native tribe, natives whose men were being pummeled into submission even if they surrendered peacefully. The Paras had been set loose. More screams, then the shouts of the Paras in return. Detective MacDonald turned back to the Saracen. Then turned and gazed from the armored vehicle to the direction of the shots. He saw the face of his son. *Planets, he was talking about planets*, thought the policeman.

Two armored cars backed onto a sidewalk at a nearby intersection and the Paras quick-marched a group of men into them. The men's arms were pinned high behind their backs and the Paras were kicking them as they hustled them along. The detective turned away from that which did not concern him.

"Bell."

"Yes, Sir."

MacDonald gestured toward an army officer with a sten gun cradled under his arm.

"Tell that officer over there to get a platoon together. Get to the top of the street, where the shooter was, and grab kids. Youngsters. Grab them and ask them if they saw the shooter. No rough stuff, but sometimes kids will blurt things out. Move quickly."

"Yes, Sir."

MacDonald hesitated, something he had caught himself doing more often lately.

"Bell!"

The young man froze in his tracks.

"They're children. Strictly by the book."

Years of this had developed in MacDonald an extra sense about these streets. Sometimes he could feel the closeness of the killers, could almost pick them out of a crowd without a word being spoken. And sometimes there was the emptiness of a frigid starry night. That was how he felt now.

He was wasting his time here. They all were. This was not the work of an ordinary Belfast lad full of hoary song and hasty instruction. This bastard was an expert. He was calculating, and he was absolutely stone cold. And, MacDonald's detective heart whispered, he was long bloody well gone.

The sniper stood before the small sink, his hands before him, fingers spread wide. He was shaking. Just a bit, but his hands were trembling, and he could feel the air pressing the soft sheen of perspiration in the small of his back.

He had been startled by them stopping, and he had fired too many shots. His rule was a maximum of two shots, but he had broken that rule, a cardinal rule, and he had broken it.

He watched the water flow into the sink, cascading onto the bar of soap, making a warm reassuring pool of cleanliness. The warm water would calm him, it always did. Pushing his hands into the sink, he thought of the ancient incantation of the Latin mass. *Lavabo*. I shall wash. That was what the priest would say before consecrating the host.

The man at the sink said the word aloud. Why had the Church abandoned its Latin and its tradition? Only trouble had followed that choice. With tradition you had the knowledge of all the generations who had come before. You could touch them. You could draw from their strength.

And the Church betrayed all that and fled Latin to the arms of English. They had discarded the language of the spirit for the language of the marketplace. And now look. The people were leaving the Church and finding only the void.

He washed carefully, slowly. He had lain in that dirty room for hours before the armored car rumbled down the street. He had willed it to stop and it did, and he had willed them to open the rear door and they did, and he had killed them for listening to his thoughts. For surely they had heard him thinking. Why else would they have come to a halt? Nothing had moved on the street, nothing had been thrown at them, no one had so much as gestured or even looked in their direction. Despite all that, they had bent to his will and done his bidding and died.

This power he had come to posses was frightening. What if others could hear his thoughts? What if he caused more vehicles to stop or people to suddenly alter their course of action? That could be chaotic. That could be very dangerous.

He dried off as carefully as he had washed, then he chose his clothing from what he had laid out on the bed.

Again he held out his hands, fingers wide, and was pleased to see the tremor had left him.

Well done said a voice, a too-loud voice inside his head that startled him.

"Thank you, Sir."

The voice didn't reply.

Leaning over the sink, coming close to the mirror, he examined his eyes and again checked his hands. He was fine. However, when he turned away from the mirror, something let him know he was not fine. He knew the voice could not be real. He had answered a voice that no one else could hear. He had not willed the men in the armored car to do anything.

He returned to the mirror, staring, touching his right hand to both cheeks, pulling down the flesh below each eye, searching. It felt like there was something there, some small thing, sometimes behind one eye, then the other. If only he could see what it was, he would feel better. He felt like it was a thing that was growing but it had not grown big enough yet for him to see it.

What if it grew while he was sleeping? What if he woke up and was blinded by this thing? How would he get home?

He went to the bed and sat down, sat at an angle from where he could see the mirror but not his reflection. That made him feel better. When he had covered the mirror with newspaper he felt much safer. Felt his mind become refreshed, felt his touch and hearing become keen, and most important, he knew his eyes were clear.

He could sense the world so much more keenly now. He was becoming someone new. You did that in life. You were a child, then a man, then you had various incarnations. That was the spiritual path. All wise people knew that. He knew it. He wasn't egotistical about it, it was just a fact. This spiritual change would take him to new places. He marveled at how quickly it had come upon him. He must continue his journey, he must be prepared for what this change would bring.

He leaned against the headboard. Tonight he would stay awake. Without sleep his mind would become even clearer, and in the morning the new sun would remove all shadows, then he would know exactly what to do. He just had to wait for the cleansing certainty of the sun, for grace, for the strength of focused will. He had been given such a gift, but now he had come to understand he was only its instrument. He whispered words to himself, saying he must remain humble, he must stay focused, he must wait for the sun.

Expecting unpleasantness, Jimmy and the detective had both been shocked by the instantaneous explosion of rage their meeting produced. It had not been arguing, it had been mindless screaming. Not accusation, but near-physical attack. The fact that it was inside an automobile made it glass-edged, more fearsome, more frightening.

Jimmy had accused the copper of murder, lying, cowardice, and had called every curse down upon him. Detective MacDonald had hollered that his passenger was a goddamn fool who could not be trusted to tie his own shoes. He had yelled that no one could guarantee anything once a raid was in progress, that each operation was a roll of the dice and everyone on both sides damn well knew it. He had yelled at Jimmy to grow up and accept responsibility. Then he had tried to calm him by saying that now Louis was safe. Safe because he was too close to Jimmy to arrest without grabbing Jimmy as well. So they were both safe. For now.

In the heat of those moments the two men had their arms raised in front of them, fists clinched, and everything they were hung in that small space between them, for if they came to blows neither one would stop. At some level they both understood that. They'd felt those flames and backed away.

MacDonald drove, gripping the wheel like he would twist it from its metal foundation and strangle it. He sat with both arms stiff, his torso pushed deep into the seat. His breathing was slow, deep and edgy, like the way they counted backward before firing a missile into space. It was lowering and intimidating.

In the passenger seat Jimmy also skirted the edge of fury. But his rage was balled up into his body, a body that was twisted away from the driver. He watched the night pass by, saw too his own reflection in the car's window, and piled upon that he saw the reflection of the driver. That image turned every so often to look at him, perhaps to make sure he was not about to attack. Even as the car slowed and came into the lights of a small shop the cop's eyes kept bouncing furtive glances off Jimmy.

MacDonald cruised into the lighted area then hit the brakes sharply. Jimmy Fitzgerald slid forward in the seat so hard he had to brace himself against the dashboard. The two exchanged a look and Jimmy knew the detective had deliberately startled him by braking so quickly, had told him in yet another unspoken way who was in control.

Taking the keys the copper went into the shop, leaving the IRA man alone in the vehicle to watch a stream of Protestants walk past. These pedestrians, if they had even an inkling of who he was would pull him from the car and kill him. They might beat him to death, might stab or shoot him, or turn him over to the local merchants of the macabre. He would not get out of here alive.

He watched the copper through the window, nonchalant with his hands in his pockets, patiently standing in line to order his carry-away. Even with the copper standing right there they could pull him out of the car, a quick question and an answer they didn't like. That would be all it would take. He stared at MacDonald, thinking, *the bastard, the fucking bastard, he knows it and he's letting me twist here.* And what made Jimmy angriest was that the little trick was working. He was silently urging the copper to place his order and get the hell out of there, to get back in the bloody car and drive away from the Shankill Road.

Bastard, Jimmy thought. Then he whispered aloud, "Burn in hell, you bastard."

Finally MacDonald came out with the food. No words were passed as he got back in and made a U-turn on the street, the aroma of food filling the vehicle. The detective ripped open the bag and proffered it at his passenger. Jimmy reached in and took a handful of chips. The food and the movement of the vehicle relaxed him enough so that he leaned back, concentrating on the food, inhaling its aroma and taking very small bites.

He could see that the copper too was less tense. He was driving with one hand now. His breathing had become silent as he fished in the bag for morsels. They headed toward the downtown area, always skirting the lines between the warring neighborhoods, always staying just inside the Protestant side.

MacDonald looked at his passenger.

"Tell me what you've heard about that sniper."

They passed an arcade, one of the city's neutral zones, a place where all sides could come to see how long they could keep a silver pinball from going down a hole.

"I keep inquirin'. I've asked everybody. Nobody knows who the fuck it is. Ya can scream at me all ya want. I'm tellin' ya. The man's a fucken' phantom, so he is."

Jimmy was surprised at how calmly MacDonald took his words. The copper stared ahead, then asked,

"What rumors do you hear about him?"

Jimmy took a piece of fried chicken from the bag. It was still very hot and he passed it among his fingers as he answered.

"He's from the Markets, he's from Ballymurphy, or Dublin, or Tipperary far away. Just a bunch of gossip far as I can see."

The copper nodded then glanced at Jimmy.

"Who do you think he is?"

Jimmy was surprised that the question flattered him, and he answered honestly.

"He's no local fella for damn sure. Dublin? It's possible. Ya know, it could be one of yours. Someone got training in the army, had a rough tour, now he hates the army. Could be a woman. Some women are crack shots. Maybe it's Annie fucken' Oakley."

Jimmy saw his sarcasm hit home. The copper gripped the wheel again and Jimmy gave the words a little twist by reaching in the bag and shoving fries in his mouth. MacDonald glared at him.

"This is no bloody joke."

Jimmy looked back then pushed a piece of chicken in with the fries.

"I want you to think," said MacDonald. "Has anyone new been in the area? Anyone who sticks out?"

The Irishman chewed slowly, thoroughly enjoying the copper's impatience and the grain of power he temporarily held over MacDonald. When he finished chewing he passed the back of his hand over his mouth.

"There's a Yank." He was silenced by a burp that wanted to come out. Pressing his chest he gasped then continued. "A Yank. He's renting a room. He's a school teacher, says he's researching his ancestors."

"A Yank," said MacDonald.

"He's leaving soon. Told me he's goin' home next week."

"Tracing his ancestors?"

"That's what he said."

The detective ran that through the flow of recent events, his talks with other suspects, the endless briefings. It was, he concluded, just stupid enough to be true. A goddamn American shows up in the middle of everything to trace the site of his ancestral hovel and the Irish piss pot that goes with it. But he would check this Yank, maybe have him arrested, shake him a bit, see what fell from the tree.

"Anyone else?"

"There's rumors of vampires."

"What?"

"Honest to Christ. It's all over. They're sayin' the Butcher

Gang are really vampires. They fell from German planes durin' the war. Now they've come to life, they're killin' Catholics. That's why no one sees 'em. They're the fucken' undead so they are."

Jimmy checked the bag but didn't pull anything out, adding.

"Some people are carryin' wooden stakes, so they are. The women are fucken' terrified, afraid to go out, crosses everywhere, holy water too. They're fucken' paralyzed with the fright."

"Vampires," said MacDonald.

"Sure as I'm sittin' here."

The detective knew the man was telling the truth. And why not believe in vampires? Five years ago he would not have believed humans capable of what he now dealt with every day.

After he dropped his passenger off he saw the logic in this new terror of the night. Of course it wasn't the people up the street, the people you passed shopping, the people who fixed the water leaking under the sidewalk. It was vampires. He wanted to believe it himself, wanted to see them turn into bats and flap through a sleeping lady's open window. That would be a comfort, that would be an awakening from this nightmare that was filled with his fellow man.

The detective drove alone through the night, reaching into the bag, frustrated that it was empty. He crushed the white paper with one hand and threw it onto the floor. Near his house he cruised around the block several times, then turned into his little street.

The parked cars were all empty, the houses, including his own, were dark. Getting out, he stopped in the street and looked around, not knowing what it was he wanted to see. Then he went inside to check messages and to leave them and to lie awake wondering at what heaven had let loose in his land.

Michaela looked at this man she had fallen in love with. Saw his scars, pain, pride, his goodness, courage, his gentle caring, the contours of his imagination, his focused masculinity.

"I love you," she said. The words made him smile, and seemed also to embarrass him, which made her care for him all the more. "I do. I just love you."

He closed his eyes to the shower of affection.

"I love you too. I loved you the first time I saw you. It was that sudden."

"That sudden?" she teased.

"Aye, it was. Didn't take a second."

She rubbed his hair and kissed him. She pressed against him, wrapping his head in one arm and pulling him close, saying, "I would think of you. Then I couldn't stop thinking of you. Then I couldn't wait to be with you. Then I thought, 'Michaela, you're in love with Jimmy Fitzgerald and that's a fact.'" They kissed. She pushed him away and bounced off the couch, speaking as she dressed.

"To celebrate you can get me a drink at the Cracked Cup. You can get me a bite to eat. An' you can ask me for a dance." Then she went to the bureau with its mirror and applied make-up and combed her hair as she again told him she loved him.

He watched her, enthralled with her voice, her body, her hair, her joy and the affection that flowed over him. He thought back, realizing he had known her just six weeks but understanding at the same moment that she had changed him, that she was sweeping him along toward something he had never known before. He was unsure of what it would be, but he knew he was changing and the reason was her. With this woman he felt like a little boy climbing a hill, sure that the answer to everything would soon be resolved with the view from the summit.

He thought of who he was and what he had become. She understood he was in the IRA and she accepted that and all the risks it brought. But what he really was lay motionless and arid within, and no woman's love had consoled that barren landscape. Only a copper knew that Jimmy Fitzgerald, only a copper's dull shoes raised dust on that secret terrain.

And the dead. They knew. They would wait for him. They would drape him with their unlived young lives. And even when he was numbered among them he would find no solace. For God and the saints might forgive, but Ireland's dead would not.

"Which do ya like?"

He started, then saw she was holding up two different pairs of earrings. He picked the pair in her left hand, a set of tiny blue sea shells. She smiled and put those on.

"Ready?" she asked.

"Ready," he answered.

As everyone did in this place, they paused before they stepped onto the sidewalk. Paused to listen, to see, to feel, to protect life. Then, holding hands they stepped off.

The crowd and the sanctuary of the Cracked Cup embraced them. Here was a pub and a social club, drink, dance and song, men, women and a sprinkling of children. Here was everything this conflict was and was about. Catholicism, Irish nationalism, pride, irreverence, quick wit, instant fury, prejudice, open wounds and secret grudges. Here was exuberant life dancing, reaching for today and tomorrow while the past called the tune.

The crowd embraced the IRA man and his love, bought

them drinks and saw how they cared so deeply for each other. The crowd saw, and the crowd rejoiced. The Irish laughed and sang and the room rocked as the people of the Lower Falls shouted to the world who they were.

Michaela danced with her man, feeling the energy of everyone present but seeing only him. Love took her and twirled her, lifted her up and spun her round with the man and the dance.

Holding her, Jimmy could forget, could briefly feel only her touch, her smile, this moment with this woman and he felt free, felt he was again simply the man he had been. He felt the boy within, with all his promise, and he felt hope. Hope that there was a way out for him, that with this woman he could be free again. With this woman he could do anything. Perhaps even look within at the man looking out.

She held a cup of hot tea, the sugar falling into it hissing in protest, fluid too hot to sip, steam twisting above the cup in warning, like the snap of an annoyed cat's tail. In her padded worn chair Michaela balanced the cup, the blouse she would sew, and her blanket. The rhythm of the needle, the pungent hot liquid, the embrace of the wool blanket worked to slow her heartbeat, to quiet her breathing.

All this served to make way for the image of the man, not that she had to summon him forth, because he permeated her now. His face was always with her, his scent, touch, embrace, his sound, his walk, his everything.

She paused to examine the ivory colored button against the blue blouse, then bit the thread in two. Working the material she thought how fast all this had happened. *Did I reach out to take him or did he pour into my cravings, to cool there, to become firm and permanent, to be part of me? Or was it simply meant to be? I believe that. It was meant to be, fate, tumbling down through time, waiting to come together, to form something new together, to create love.*

Holding up the blouse, she decided what skirt she would wear with it, what lunch she would have in this outfit, what shoes would go best.

"Jimmy." She said it aloud, drawing the blanket tighter at all the forces his name conjured. The IRA—frightening, thrilling, captivating, merciless, brave, tough, brilliant. Jimmy. There was all of that, but she and Jimmy were separate from it. That was the world outside. What they had was inside, unspoken, undeclared, needing no proclamation, no unfurling flag.

In school didn't they teach us that the core of the Earth is a hot molten ball? Thousands of degrees it is, only peeking out now and then through a volcano. Yet we drifted atop that inferno with our cool water, soothing breezes, gentle rains. Jimmy and I are like that. We will float on all the turmoil, float apart from the cauldron of hate and conflict, and we will survive. No, we will thrive.

I'm scared. I'm too small, too weak, too selfish, too lazy. I'm only a girl.

The way they respect him; the knowing nods, the whispers, they're whispering about me too now. The girl at his side, holding his hand, his gaze, making him laugh, they're watching. I like that. Am I too proud? No, it's nice, it's just nice.

And all that goes on. Dear God. Bombs, shootings, black masks and death. No, don't think that. You love him. That's all there is. The other things are the outside world. They are not us. Not Jimmy, not really. They are just things that have to happen. And they will. Our love will flow around those things, it will grow wider, and those other things will not matter.

She told herself this, but still each local action ricocheted through her, chilled her, pushed and pulled, not stopping until she saw him again and she could start over.

Then reunion, where all direction vanished as she fell into the deepening circle around him, his arms holding her, his arms the source of everything. They never discussed what happened outside, not once. They both knew, so what was the point of mere words?

This unspoken thing between them feeding her longing, Jimmy drenched in what had happened outside, she pressing a finger to his lips, then the two of them floating. Just one finger so gently to his lips. *Don't speak, don't speak, lovely boy. Let me take all of that and keep it within. Don't speak, close your eyes, feel us float above all that froths and burns. See how we float above all of it? Do you see? It is all so clear, do you see? You must. Do you see?*

All of the chaos outside came to settle beneath Louis's chest, a warm intruder who curled up there, banishing day and night, replacing them with dim vision, dull thoughts and ever-gnawing fear. These things came after they told him he was to replace Big Mick, and he was to find a replacement for Tommy Higgins. It was now he who would choose when, where and what to strike. Big Mick had worn this mantle as if born to carry it. Louis accepted it with humility and dread. He felt like a tyke trying on his da's shoes and hat, thrilled at the attire but wondering how he could ever grow into it.

And if his thoughts ran away, he saw himself in a high walled courtyard where all that stood was himself and every day he had left on earth. So he did not let his thoughts run away. He didn't tell his wife of the promotion, but she knew something had changed and she probably guessed what it was. Part of their strength was knowing what to discuss and what to leave unsaid. And this they would leave unsaid, knowing their silent bond needed only a glance or passing touch to grow stronger.

As the days dripped past, he received more instructions. Code words, phone numbers, and he learned of more safe houses and hidden weapons caches.

Two weeks after being tapped for command he called the unit together, the two new members and Jimmy. The new ones had earned their stripes by running errands, moving weapons, rioting, relaying messages, standing up to British beatings, and keeping their mouths shut.

Michael Wright, 20, had blonde hair, was a wiry five foot ten with muscular arms, an intense gaze, strong jaw and a reputation as a man very good with his fists. Peter Riordan, aka Black Peter, was lean, hard, five foot seven with an infectious grin, brown eyes, and was known to be fearless in the face of British troopers, armored cars and gunfire. At twenty-three his black hair was as long and wild as a San Francisco hippie, and he was calm as syrup. Behind them Jimmy slouched in a chair, hands folded like a schoolboy waiting for an exam to be handed out.

Clearing his throat, Louis outlined his plan. There would be foot patrols about today, and he wanted to use two automobiles to ambush them. One car would be weaponless and the men in it would act as scouts. The other would have a driver, and a passenger who would be armed with a Lewis machine gun.

He saw their eyebrows go up. The Lewis was a World War I weapon. Its wide barrel had a large circular ammunition holder and the deadly weapon rested on a tripod. Everyone in the world had seen it used. It was the machine gun on the airplanes that knocked King Kong off the Empire State building.

"If it was good enough for King Kong it's sure as fuck good enough for the Brits," Louis told them. That got a nervous laugh from all of them and Louis quickly added, "You new fellas will scout. If they stop ya, yer just out lookin' for girls like. Then let us know where they are. Any questions?"

There were no questions and Riordan and Wright departed. Their engine coughed, seized, came to life again, stopped with a backfire, then turned over. Louis and Jimmy heard the car bounce off the curb as the driver made a U-turn on the narrow street below, rubber belts squealing, the smell of exhaust coming through the window.

"There's a Leeson Street car," said Louis.

"Aye," his companion replied, adding, "Built for smooth getaways."

They both smiled, then Jimmy asked,

"Why the Lewis?"

His leader shrugged.

"It was available and it puts the fear of God in the Brits."

Louis looked at his companion for several moments before asking,

"How's Michaela?"

"Fine, she's fine."

"Smashin' woman, so she is."

"Aye. Can't figure what she sees in me."

"No one else can either."

They laughed out loud, both relaxing just a bit, leaning back in their chairs.

"Think you'll marry, then?"

"Jesus, Louis, I don't know. Marriage an' me. I don't know."

"Best thing a man can do. Marry a good woman, have children. Nothin' better for a man."

Jimmy nodded, folded his hands and unfolded them.

"I've thought of it."

"Good, that's good then."

They let the silence rest in the room a bit, then Louis got up, split the thin curtains with one hand and peered out.

"Anythin'?" asked Jimmy.

"Not a peep."

Louis stood by the window, occasionally touching the curtain, once balling a portion of it in his fist and cursing low.

"We have a solid source. They should've been along by now."

They heard the car again pass by below, moving slowly as it took a nearby corner. They all knew the longer the vehicle moved around the area, the more vulnerable it became to British notice.

"Maybe they cancelled the patrols," said Jimmy.

Louis didn't turn, but shook his head no. Again his hand

touched the curtain and he said,

"We've a source inside. The patrols are on, she's certain."

Jimmy's surprise caused him to ask,

"She?"

Realizing he'd said too much, Louis turned.

"I shouldn't have said that. It's not to leave this room."

"I understand."

"We've a girl workin' for the Brits at Royal Avenue. Got access to their operational reports. Everything in triplicate, ya know the Brits. She types it. Worth her weight in gold."

"I'll be damned. Inside the place?" asked Jimmy.

"Bug in a rug she is, got the courage alright."

They were interrupted by feet running up the stairs, and Wright bounded into the room.

"Twelve-man patrol comin' up the other side a' Divis Flats, got a Saracen wanderin' around too."

"Good lads."

"Stick to me, Jimmy," Louis said as they trotted down the stairs, outside and around a corner to a blue Cortina.

Louis pointed for Jimmy to drive as two teenagers appeared, carrying the Lewis. They struggled to get the machine gun into the back seat, then plunked the weapon awkwardly on Louis like a fat blind date.

Jimmy worked the gears, grinding one and whispering obscenities as they picked up speed. Twice they made an oval through the area, exchanging glances with the young scouts at key intersections. On the third loop a red-headed boy stepped away from a corner wall, signaling.

He pointed in an arc, then put four fingers to his right, and with both hands held eight fingers aloft to his left. Louis waved at the boy, who disappeared down an alley. He leaned forward, putting a hand on Jimmy's shoulder.

"We'll make one pass at 'em. Try to hit the lot," he said.

"Got it."

"Ready, Mate?"

"Ready."

Now the world turned to slow motion as they came around the corner to a wide waste ground area and Jimmy saw the patrol strung out, wide white eyes staring, weapons rising at the sight of a vehicle emerging from the Lower Falls. He saw each face, saw two not comprehend, saw eight dive for cover, saw two drop to one knee and fire at the very moment Louis did.

The Lewis walloped Jimmy's consciousness, screeched blue and white inside his head. He drove as slowly as he dared. The man in the back screamed at the top of his lungs as the Brits disappeared in the weapon's smoky recoil and the dust raised by the slugs, death stomping its feet all around them. A splash of red blew upward, then was swallowed by the dust as Louis shouted, "Go!"

They stared at the shattered windscreen as familiar streets spun past, the vehicle screeched to a halt near teenage boys, who jumped in the car as the men got out. The two men trotted down a block then into an alley, and were in a safe house seconds before an armored car roared past. It clanged to a halt and they could hear shouts, then bottles smashing off the Saracen. The vehicle's engine whined as it backed up, went forward again then raced down another street, striking out blindly at the tormentors of the British Army.

The British radios were frantic with messages, armored cars were coming, a helicopter as well. In barracks throughout the city Tommys were racing for weapons and gear. They would grab the Lower Falls by the throat and kick its damned Irish ass. They would shake it and spit in its face. But they would not find the two men in this little room, nor the weapon skinny boys buried beneath smooth dirt and stones.

In the waste ground the blood and dust would grow dark together and the young English boy, who had no more blood to give this land, would ride silently home to Coventry.

As always, Jimmy's fingertips reacted to the touch of the money envelope, the cash shouting beneath his clothing, crinkling in protest with every footfall. He had told the copper about the ambush, the Lewis, the girl on the inside, the leaping spray of red as the rounds found flesh and marrow.

They were sitting opposite one another in a cheap breakfast restaurant with high booths. The copper always chose where to meet, and he always chose cheap. Jimmy watched the copper's reaction. The man was very pleased with the information and completely indifferent to the soldier's death. The indifference wasn't feigned. *He doesn't care.* Jimmy realized. *He doesn't give a damn about the English soldiers. Christ, we have more sympathy for the poor bastards than he does.*

"What about the sniper?"

Jimmy started. MacDonald had caught him daydreaming. Jimmy leaned closer to the man, snapping,

"I told ya what I know. What I know I tell ya, do ya fucken' understand?"

The detective slowly leaned back, nodding his head. He kept nodding when a waitress asked if they would like anything else. Jimmy told the woman he was all set but the copper never even looked at her. He only stared at Jimmy, seeming to reach back to a part of himself he kept locked, a part that was primordial, and he just stared. Jimmy fidgeted as his heart jumped, the copper's soft whisper scaring him even more.

"You listen to me, you fuck. I own you. Now you think of this. You think of the Paras hitting your little lady's home at 2 a.m. after being told she'd lured one of their lads to his death. You picture her on the floor of a barracks. You picture her in a strip search. You picture her in a secret court on her way to the worst shithole in Britain. Then you watch your fucking mouth when you speak to me."

"I understand."

"Good, Jimmy. It's good that you understand." MacDonald let his words settle over the other man, then he added, "You're a book. Every time we meet, I turn the page. Whether or not there's a happy ending, well, that's up to you."

The waitress brought the bill and MacDonald left a small tip, and the two men went outside. As MacDonald walked away Jimmy ran after him, calling his name. The copper turned and Jimmy almost banged into him.

"Louis is still safe, right?"

"Right, Jimmy. Louis is still safe." The copper paused. "As long as you stick to the rules, he's safe." With that MacDonald turned and disappeared around a corner.

Jimmy watched the spot where he vanished, understanding that the copper had the only copy of the rule book, and that Jimmy was playing at night on a darkened field, with empty stands, in a game with no breaks in the action.

What the American loved about a pint of Guinness was its unhurried birth, coming so slowly from the tap, just a bit, just a bit, just a bit more. Then it stated that it had absolutely nothing better to do than be your friend.

He was on his second when someone tapped him on the shoulder.

"How ya keepin', Yank?"

"Pretty good, Louis, pretty good."

The Irishman slid onto a stool and gestured at the barman. The barman nodded and started on a pint of Guinness for Louis.

"Be with us a bit more, will ya?"

"Maybe two weeks."

Louis nodded. The American sensed the Irishman's seriousness, felt a growing presence to him, a falling back of the other men close by. It was like they'd all gone deaf, like they might all just up and float out the door with the cigarette smoke of this place.

Louis drummed the fingers of one hand on the bar as he watched the barman. He drummed very slowly, light notes, as he hummed to himself, hummed until his pint came and the barman went to the other end of the bar.

"Tell me about Vietnam."

Louis spoke to their images in the mirror, then turned to the American.

"What surprised ya most about the place?"

Louis observed the man tighten his grip on the glass before the Yank spoke.

"Myself."

"And how would that be?"

"How fast I adapted. How easy it all came to me."

Louis nodded, and sipped.

"Now that's an interesting thing. Ya know there's nothin' like speakin' to one who's been to a place for the special perspective."

They drank, the two men in the mirror awaiting the next move.

"An' now you're here."

"Right."

"Checkin' up on the ancestors."

"Right."

"An' what have ya learned?"

"They were poor."

Louis smiled, looked at the American.

"Not much research needed there, I suppose."

"Very little."

Louis eyes moved left to right and back, the mirror gave him a full view of the room. He seemed satisfied with what he saw.

"Yank, I respect ya for goin' to Vietnam. An' I respect ya for comin' here. We don't get a lot of visitors."

"Thanks, I really like the people here."

"An' when was it you was leavin'"?

"Two weeks, maybe sooner."

Louis took a drink, passed his wrist across his mouth then spoke.

"Sooner would be better."

"You think so?"

"I do."

The American took two deep draughts of the liquid, felt it in him, blinked, and leaned on one elbow.

"My schedule's pretty flexible."

Louis pulled out a pack of cigarettes, saying, "Dublin's a fine place. Lots to do."

"I've heard that."

They sat for several minutes.

"Been down to them Southern states, Yank? Alabama, Louisiana, them places?"

"Yes, I have."

"I'd love to ride a steamboat on the Mississippi."

"Maybe you will, Louis."

Another smile from the Irishman as the Yank drained his glass.

"Can I buy you another, Louis?"

"No, Yank, I'm set."

The American got up as Louis extended his hand, catching the American off guard with his strength and the pull that brought them so close.

"Thanks, Yank, now goodbye."

The intensity of Louis's gaze was as surprising as his grip. The American nodded, the Irishman released his hold and watched the Yank vanish into the night.

Louis then looked around the bar in mutual understanding that no one had seen or heard a thing.

Sergeant Albert Roberts was out of the Saracen and running before the vehicle stopped. Banging open the door of Wright's Rooming House he was greeted with a shout of "Jesus!" from Jean Wright, who had been doing a crossword puzzle while seated at her work desk near the entrance.

"Where's the American?" demanded the sergeant.

Gaping at the angry men in combat gear who had materialized among her Waterford crystal, crucifixes and white lace, Jean Wright gasped, "Gone."

"Gone where?"

The widow made small circles with both hands.

"I don't know. He was to be here 'til Friday, but day before yesterday he left. Not even a goodbye. Though he was a quiet fella like, very pleasant, helped me with the dishes so he did."

"Where's his room?"

One hand at her throat, Jean Wright stood in an empty room with five heavily armed men who seemed ready to strangle the room's emptiness, staring at her and at each other. She didn't move as they lifted the mattress, crawled into closets, checked under the sink and behind the mirror, then unscrewed the overhead light and peered into its wired foundation. When each soldier finished his task, the uniformed men stared at her as if awaiting an explanation of this walled void.

"He was a school teacher," she croaked at the little group. Getting only silence, she added, "geography and mathematics." One of the soldiers, Keith Wyeth, 19, seemed impressed and nodded his head, so she added, "Very well spoken he was, could talk on any subject. A great admirer of Gandhi he was."

"Gandhi?" asked the sergeant, almost spitting the word.

Putting her hands down Jean Wright replied, "Well, he admired Gandhi. Told me non-violence was the correct road. Thoreau, Gandhi, King. Those were his favorite men."

She spoke to the soldier who had nodded earlier. He seemed enthralled by her talk.

"Thoreau was an American who in the eighteen-hundreds built a little cabin and lived all alone at a lake for a year. Relied on himself alone, he did. Imagine. Simplify, simplify. That's what Mister Thoreau taught, all alone at his lake. Good advice, I'd say."

Sergeant Roberts turned to see his whole squad engrossed in the widow's tale.

Almost whispering, the woman added, "Wouldn't pay taxes on a war against England because he thought it unjust. Went to jail for that belief, so he did."

Two of the soldiers gaped at this news and their sergeant saw a threat to discipline.

"Search the other rooms!" he shouted, as he grabbed one squadie by the shoulder, propelling the man into the hallway.

Like infantry housewives, they peeked beneath beds, in linen closets, inspected curtains, shook boxes and examined their contents, rolled up the corners of rugs, opened refrigerators and looked into stoves. They found nothing.

The warriors and the widow tromped back downstairs. Gesturing for her to sit behind her desk, Sergeant Roberts, his squad clustered about him, said to Jean Wright, "Tell me more about this fellow."

The woman closed her eyes to focus and came up with all she could.

"He was tall and quiet. Remind you a bit of Gary Cooper, he would. Didn't smoke, took the drink but what man doesn't? Helped me with the dishes, would carry in my groceries, read three newspapers every day, so he did. Books too. Any book about, he'd pick it up and examine it and could talk on the subject matter. Said he missed his baseball, his team is the Red Sox of Boston and their enemy is the Yankees of New York. Talked one night about what he called forced busing. Said the government made all the white and black kids in Boston switch schools and ride yellow busses to other schools and there was going to be hell to pay for it. Strongest language I ever heard him use. *'There's going to be hell to pay,'* he said of all the riding about on the yellow busses. Can't say I understood what the point of it was supposed to be."

Private Wyeth, still closely following her stories asked,

"Do the yellow busses take them home as well?"

"Goodness," said Jean Wright, "I didn't think to ask him that." The private and the widow frowned at the floor as they pondered where the yellow busses might have left the kids.

And that was the information Sergeant Albert Roberts gave to Detective Ian MacDonald about the American visitor who had come, and by all appearances, gone.

"Thank you, Sergeant. Appears a bit of a wild goose chase."

"Appears so, Sir."

The detective didn't make a formal report about the reason for searching Wright's property. He did, however, file it in that part of his mind where he kept odds and ends, the stray pieces of the vast puzzle of this place. Sometimes a piece would suddenly fit and bring along with it a good portion of what had before been unseen. He would wait, and he would keep this little piece within reach.

The announcer's voice echoed off the enclosing wall of faces, faces that constantly turned to see and affirm this place, this refuge, this temple of their fathers.

"Ladies and gentlemen," the metallic speaker's voice intoned, "boys and girls," The voice paused for effect then requested, "please stand and join us in singing our national anthem."

The crowd stilled, ten thousand caps were doffed, a silence thick as the manicured grass of the infield came over the ballpark. The organ played, the people sang their anthem, they applauded their country, their voices, their town, their team, and then well-satisfied, they sat.

Above the cool hollow of an entrance to the right field grandstand, close to where the yellow pole declared fair from foul, the man back from Belfast sat alone. The hands that had held the scoped rifle were now holding a beer, massaging the wax cup, feeling its give, folding around the drink. Then with both hands he lifted it to his lips, like a priest his gold chalice.

He heard the thoughts of the crowd as a pulsating distant roar, like the noise of unseen ocean surf at night. Powerful, dangerous, with fast cross currents and hisses of invisible, angry, exploding white spray. He could deflect that sea of thought, that taking of life's measure in teaspoons, that murmur of suburban castrati. He could concentrate on this twilight doubleheader and he could take in the Yankee outfielders.

Such worthy opponents. So haughty and skilled, so calm in their enemy garb, their honed physiques, their perfect focus.

How could anyone from Boston hate them? They were beautiful in their opposition, perfect in their collective presence, and like the devils Jesus had cast out, their name was legion. The Yankees. Imagine just for a season to be one. Hated and feared wherever you set foot, having souls wax and wane with your slightest disturbance, your smallest limp, the tight flexing of a bothered hand.

Squeezing the wax cup between his knees he pressed both palms to his face, the images of Ireland flashing, the smell of the rifle's discharge, the frozen horror on faces held in the scope, those white faces looking wide-eyed but not seeing, screaming but not being heard, living and instantly dead. He relaxed his hands and raised the beer, swallowing almost all of it, letting it flow into his blood, his soul, before ordering another from the man all soft and tanned in the white apron at Fenway. He had not slept the night before or the night before that, but now he was refreshed. The thoughts of those nearby pressed one side of his head, and he put a hand there and the intrusion stopped.

The lead-off batter for the Yankees took his place in the batter's box, tapping both shoes with the bat, checking the fluttering flag and its message of the breeze.

That breeze blew into the faces of the fielders, washed over the crowd in the bleachers and down to the streets of Boston. It pressed the city, brushing South Boston, its lace-curtained windows where shy red-headed girls dreamed of love, and touched their hardened brothers on street corners, boys poised to take offense at any slight, ready to fight the very air they breathed without understanding why.

Then the air hit the chill Atlantic whose fingers pressed the city in ten score of coves, channels, and inlets, joined other currents of air crossing the water, skimming the awful currents of Fundy and on over the open waters to Ireland's fields where a man growing stiff with arthritis read the note about the returned rifle and then threw it into a turf fire. He poked the note, jabbing its black curling fist with an iron, then leaned back to caress his warm whiskey and his close leaning dog.

Above the grim city of Belfast the wind touched hills where the offspring of Jimmy Fitzgerald's rabbit hopped, listening to drying leaves whisper their wisdom. Down past the IRA graves the breeze spread, touching headstones to reassure the boys below. They heard and they agreed, and the wind fell downward to the streets of the Falls. It disturbed a thousand embers of hijacked trucks, their black skeletons glowing newly red with the gift of oxygen.

Monkey too felt the wind, a warm meat hook wrapped around his thick neck as he waited for his mates. He paused to listen to the night and grew restless to hear the wailing of the next one he pulled into the van. He saw his mates emerge from the warehouse, saw them nod as they tucked their pistols into their belts, and Monkey leaned into the open side door and began to rock.

When the van rolled away it tilted this way and that, accompanying the dance of the man with the hook. Lights out it arrived at the edge of the Catholic neighborhood and it settled, as did the men inside. Grateful for the breeze they opened windows and let the night grow all around them. What was dark within them merged with the night and the flowing breeze and Monkey rocked the vehicle. He leaned out and sniffed the wind to call in a hoarse whisper for his prey to come closer.

Two teenage boys walking on a sidewalk peered at the still van and then looked silently at one another. Neither dared admit fear, neither slowed his pace, they only drew their hands into loose fists and strode with all the purpose they could muster for a stroll to buy cigarettes. Only dogs reacted to the muffled single cry of the one the hook did not strike. He never got the chance to call again, and very slowly the van turned and retraced its route, all the while swaying as if to a song from trade winds, winter sunshine and white beaches.

Laurie Drumlin was the prettiest girl in her neighborhood, then the prettiest one in school, and now the loveliest girl at work. Laurie's warmth, her optimistic outlook, her genuine concern for people radiated from her. Those traits made her lovely face with its flawless skin, her beautiful teeth, her exquisite figure, her soft voice all the more alluring. Her hair was an arresting mix of blonde with slight red highlights, hair that women would touch and speak of with envy, hair that men would simply stare at. And her quick humor, so disarming in one so pretty, made her charm an intoxicant. For as a wise man once proclaimed: "A witty woman is a treasure. A witty beauty is a power."

And Laurie felt her power. Felt it in the way doors opened, literally and figuratively, for her. Felt it in the way service people always seemed to wait on her first, auto mechanics waved off the cost of small jobs, and other women seemed always ready to confide in her. And men. Well, men wanted what they wanted of course, but they also loved to talk to the pretty Laurie. And they wanted to impress her. They wanted Laurie to remember them, to know they were brave, to not forget they had special knowledge, secret power, as well as the knowledge of what levers to pull to initiate secret mechanizations.

Belfast was full of such men. Dangerous men, exciting men, handsome and bold, men who would lay down their lives in defense of Laurie. She loved those men, those hard men of the IRA. And that love made it possible to endure the suffocating touch of those other men. Made it easier to look into their eyes and feign wonderment at their masculinity, their good-ness, their easy contempt for everything the beautiful girl held close to her heart. Their army hired her and loved her, and she brought the soldiers cookies she made herself, she asked after them when they had colds, she looked into their eyes and just barely touched her cool fingers to their warm arms and that was enough.

For many long months she worked for them. Shutting her-self off from the ones she truly held dear, shunning every as-pect of the people and movement that gave her life its meaning.

All so she could move among the others. With their too loud haw-haw laughs, their frantic attempts at seduction, their bristling superiority, their mocking of her God and her beloved saints.

At length the others forgot she was not of their blood, their code, their desperate need for rules to queue up for, and social classes to bow down to.

But Laurie never forgot. Her God and saints were always close by, a silent prayer away, closer than the closest touch of the frenetic enemy. She rose among them and they trusted her more, and she typed their mundane reports and discerned from them the flesh and blood reality those smudged reports would send to her childhood's lovely lanes and alleyways. And discreetly, expertly, she passed that information on to the orga-nization that was her only love, and the men within it moved to meet the invaders and justice was done. Afterward she would see the pain on the ruddy close-shaved faces of the officers, and then she would read the report.

As Laurie was typing she noticed movement, noticed a man in civilian clothes enter the room, pause, look around then come to her desk. She looked up. The visitor was of medium height, had a strong build, and seemed to find basic social skills a strain as he asked,

"I'm looking for Colonel Fitz-Mallory."

Laurie smiled and pointed.

"End of the hall, second door on the left."

"Thank you."

"You're welcome, Sir."

Laurie glanced up as the man walked off and she knew exactly what he was, his accent, his arrogance, his gagging condescension. *Copper.* The man vanished around the corner, and Laurie, who always tried to avoid cursing aloud, could not help the words that seared within her. *You special branch fucker.*

Detective Ian MacDonald stayed less than ten minutes in the office of Colonel Thomas Fitz-Mallory. Leaving, he nodded pleasantly to the pretty woman and she nodded back. Then he was gone, and Laurie made a mental note to herself to record the time and date. No piece of information was too small, no detail too remote for the tapestry an oppressed people were weaving.

The beautiful woman returned to her typing, then checked the colonel's letter of condolence for spelling or grammatical errors. There were none, and she carefully set the tome at the left corner of her desk. It told two grieving parents of their son's bravery, his dedication, the respect with which he was held by all his comrades and officers. It did not speak of the cause of death, just the specialness of the life lost.

Laurie had typed many such letters before. Letters that would find their way to vine-embraced cottages in Yorkshire villages, smoky, damp walk-ups in the industrial midlands, and occasionally the rolling grounds of the gentry. No matter how plain the language, no matter how simple and declarative the typed sentences, the letters would provoke anguished questions. For every summoning up of a young life, for every bullet cutting through camouflaged cloth and all that lay beneath, for every bomb set and delivered among uniformed young men, loved ones would sob and ask why. They would be told there was no answer, it was God's will.

But Laurie's heart had a simple answer, and if those families, friends and comrades had asked, she would tell them that answer: *Get out of my country.*

Slouched against the passenger door Louis felt a new calm, an easing into command. He had become used to having others react to his slightest instructions, their efforts to anticipate his moods. He had learned to keep his own counsel, learned to ration out his words, become used to the others falling silent at his entry. The new commander saw them seek their own courage in his steadiness, find their cause in his righteous fury, and he came to see he could mold their fright and twist it to his purpose.

And now he had single-handedly drawn up this bombing blitz, this peek-a-boo flirtation with death and destruction. His team was to move in coordination with a series of coded warnings.

"We will be like surfers catching those big waves in Hawaii," Louis told them. Catch the wave correctly and no one would get hurt, let alone killed. Catch that blue wall of water and a piece of the enemy's economic infrastructure would tumble down. Buildings would fall into the street, petrol stations would rage in flames, a car dealership would be no more, a little knick-knack store owned by a very militant Unionist would shatter to little white ceramic pieces, peeping their last on the black motorway.

Then as effortless as a glance the plan had unrolled. A single driver with the bomb leaving the car at the target and instantly hopping into the getaway van. *One-two-three-four.* Like that Beatles song. The bomb vehicle placed, the driver to the getaway car, a man nearby telephoning the correct word, the team vanishing into the traffic. *One-two-three-four.* And the explosions tore at the nerves and heart of the enemy, bursting white smoke, a hurtling boom pushing through a thousand chest cavities, then another bomb, and another and another.

As fast as it began, it was over, and at the safe house every one of them stared at their commander and he shouted their names, rubbed their heads, slapped their backs. Louis hugged them and could have kissed them, because today they'd shown the bastards, and the team looked at their leader and every man loved him.

This was leaping joy, a blessed and a holy thing, to get up off the floor where all your life they had walked on you, walked on your father long dead, and on your mother, God rest her soul. Walked on everything in you and about you and wiped their feet and smirked at the dirt that clung to you. But by Jesus you got up off that floor and you showed them, you scared the shit out of them, yes you did boy, and who was smirking, and who was on the floor now?

Then, like monks done with their chants, the solemn men filed from their hiding place, heads down in the soft rain, with the water just beginning to gather itself by the curbs, just commencing to nudge aside the cigarettes and the candy wrappers. The men stepped over the running water as the rain increased, then silent and gentle as Irish mist, the IRA was gone.

Jimmy had known this time would come, this moment of confession, when he would pull off the mask and let Michaela see all that dwelt beneath. As he approached her across the room he felt like a man trying to walk on ten-foot crutches, wanting to go forward but able only to swing helplessly as his strength drained away. She saw.

"Jimmy, what is it?"

"I'm not who you think I am."

Michaela felt her legs weaken, her chest squeeze tight, she brought her hands up for balance, the floor suddenly gone wobbly. The depth of his misery yawned before her adding to the sense that what she stood upon was dissolving, was turning into something that could pull her down and smother her. A soft pink blush touched the bottom of both sides of her jaw as she said,

"Then tell me who you are."

So he did. He spoke of his induction into the secret army, the pride, the fear, the brotherhood. His final arrest, of how something broke within, his falling into despair. He spoke of his humiliation, of being curled in a ball, feeling his manhood run from him, of betraying brave men he loved. Jimmy spoke of the burning shame, the terror sparked by a casual glance, the deep hollow blackness that now dwelt within. Of how with each awakening there came a knot of shame in his stomach and of how he and that knot greeted each new day.

Michaela teetered, took half a step back, her color draining, clearing her throat once, then again.

"Alright," she managed to say. "We...we'll be alright."

She reached out to touch his face.

"Jimmy, we'll be alright. I promise."

They sat in chairs opposite one another, the chairs close, the man and woman leaned closer, as she came to understand that he had no plan beyond telling her. No idea of what to do next. He'd talked and talked, pacing as he gesticulated. And then he was gone, leaving her to mull this thing alone. He left her with none in whom she could confide, with no special friend's special advice, no one to whisper even the emptiest of reassurances.

Later, deep in her cushioned chair, eyes closed, breathing slow, her fingers explored the inside of her purse. She felt the soft pack of cigarettes, the stark dimensions of a matchbook. Inhaling the smoke she recalled the riots, the fear, her sudden discovery of the iron within herself. And, she thought, while so many had killed, while mobs had raged and the injured fell and staggered all around, she had harmed no one. She had healed and protected, had sheltered life from hate's whirlwind.

I'm a healer she thought. *Not a saint, maybe not even a very good person. But I can heal. I will do that. I can love and I love him. I will heal his wound. He'll be whole and walking free again. I'll stand with him no matter what.*

I'm afraid, yes I am. I'm afraid of all the boots and guns, the fists and the loud voices. Yes I am, I'm very afraid, but I will not abandon him. He's a man. No more, no less. A woman's love can save a man. I love him. That's all I need to know. I love him, I trust him, I believe in him.

Michaela let the cigarette lie on her lips, as she breathed in and breathed out. Her eyes remained closed, her chest rising, falling. Her left hand, holding the cigarette, touched the ashtray and she flipped the gray ash.

She could not see the path over these harsh hills but she could see the lovely valley beyond. She would simply keep walking, and she and Jimmy would reach that far green place.

Smoking the butt down to its nub she opened her eyes and crushed out the cigarette. Then she rose to run hot water at the sink because lately she had been lazy and there were many dishes to be washed.

Laurie Drumlin never had to write anything down. It was a blessing to have such a memory, such a clean, crisp image of so many pages, such precise recall of hand-drawn maps and hasty scribbles in the margins. And, ever playing the wide-eyed girl, she had always paid rapt attention to the army officers trying to thrill her with the arcane details of their profession.

Kill zones, interlocking fields of fire, L-shaped ambushes, turning the enemy's flank, grids, coordinates. Blinking, she would feign amazement, focusing, she would remember every detail.

Now on the white stationery before her she immediately saw opportunity, saw justice waiting to be meted out. This plan told of a secret observation post to be set inside a vacant house on a little dead-end street. A place where, once in, there was only one way out. She knew the street, and the high land nearby with low buildings from where Irish patriots could look down on the English interlopers. She'd even pointed out the risk to a captain, who'd smiled, winked and replied,

"Don't worry dearie, it'll be very quick. We'll be in and away in two days. We'll catch Paddy asleep in his little bed."

Sounds of a fiddle and tin whistle waxed and waned with each opening of the pub door. Cigarette smoke too peeked out into the night, wafting past the pretty girl in the trench coat with the wide belt and simple knot.

The men she spoke to leaned forward to hear her soft voice, could not help the glances that took her in with the information she provided. She saw their glances and didn't mind, for they were as lovely as were ever any men who lived. They were our lads, our dignity, our justice, our courts and our police.

With a wide smile she went over the whole English plan one more time, and they nodded and now they too had a firm grasp of it. As they slipped back into the night, they were gone so suddenly she didn't know if they'd heard her whispered, "God bless."

Nolan Street was a small finger poking into the surrounding rows of houses. Its three dozen dwellings, three abandoned with windows shut by nailed plywood, were like the others in the Falls. They wore their years openly, paint faded, roofs bowed, their little yards with their sturdy little commodes. This little side street was unremarkable, dead-end, small, and few people came and went from it, this place not quite inside the Falls Road encampment, this little place that had always somehow been apart.

But today it held unwavering interest for two men coming separately on bicycles and a third strolling past, pausing only to light his pipe, and then moving on. The next day at a different time the men returned, they checked the wheel of one bike, tipped their hats to a passing mother and child. And they went on their way.

Other men watched too. These men were blocks away, secreted in rooms they had entered using their potpourri of master keys. The men crouched perfectly still, peering into small telescopes, their fit bodies easily meeting the challenge of their posture.

These men were patient. These men, when set to a goal, let nothing deter them. Those traits had carried them through brutal training, through a physical and psychological ordeal designed to make normal men quit. Almost all the hopefuls had yielded, but not these men. Their skills were myriad, their focus absolute, their fierce pride unspoken.

These men were Britain's Strategic Air Services. The SAS.

Through a day and a night, silent and unmoving as amber, they had waited. And now they were watching the IRA watch the little dead end street.

When the pipe smoker stopped at the street, the man at the telescope moved his hand to the button of a radio strapped to his chest. Without speaking he pressed the receiver down for three seconds. This told the others watching that here was our prey. The radio, its volume barely audible, hissed back with three short bursts of static, saying *yes, we see him too.* The procedure was repeated with the men on the bikes, as a camera clicked and the men in the room stayed motionless.

The next day Laurie Drumlin sat up straight in the big chair in the colonel's office, smiling as the accolades fell over her. Colonel Fitz-Mallory was not one for empty praise. When he said something he meant it. Beside him, Captain Nolan nodded in cadence with the colonel's every word. Laurie was to be promoted, a significant raise, a lot more responsibility, some special training outside London. Mum's the word.

Laurie glowed. She asked the colonel if he was sure she was ready for this assignment. Absolutely, he assured her. She'd earned it, she was invaluable. They would leave tomorrow, be back in four or five days.

"Might even get to play the tourist," he joked.

Laurie decided to keep this completely to herself. She didn't know the details yet, but information here was not only power, it was life and death. She would keep her own counsel and go to England. That night, beneath the crucifix over her bed in her flat near the university, Laurie prayed for the wisdom to make the right choices, for strength to meet the challenges of the new assignment, and she prayed in thanks to God for giving her this opportunity.

In the morning she packed a single bag with two changes of clothes and the accoutrements of a young woman. Then she said a final silent prayer and was off. The trip in the plane was very quick, with a small meal and only a short stroll into the operation center of the airbase. Laurie was standing slightly behind the colonel and the captain, feeling very happy, when two burly women with pistols and flak jackets took her by each arm and steered her away.

"Get off!" she shouted.

But no one even turned to look at her. The colonel and the captain just kept walking straight ahead as the young Irish woman was manhandled into a small cinderblock cubicle. Four hours later, her nose bleeding, her face red with welts, fear and rage, she was still there. Not a word had been spoken to her, and all she could see where the thick ankles and regulation shoes of the women who had beaten her.

But there was a sound. It was the cacophony of her own thoughts screaming at her, presenting a thousand horrors, a myriad of accusations. As she waited, the second hand of the clock in her head emitted a shout with each and every one of its movements. And Laurie understood, that the longer they left her alone, the more they were comfortable with what they already knew, very comfortable.

Slowly the blood from her nose congealed on her lips and chin, stopping its drip on her white blouse. And while her body struggled to heal itself, in her mind what she had caused to be let loose in Belfast kept up its banshee cry.

Shedding his clothes and leaving them on a chair, Louis Duffy slid beneath the blanket to press close to his wife, who cried out,

"Jesus, your feet are like ice."

"Warm 'em up, then!" said Louis pressing closer, as his wife announced,

"Put yer socks on, you'll give me pneumonia. God ya must be part polar bear."

"Ah, me secret's out." He gently bit her shoulder, setting her to laughing and sliding beneath the covers whispering,

"Stop it, the kids'll think we're daft."

He didn't answer but slid an arm around her waist, pulling her very close and kissing her cheek. She turned and pressed her face to his shoulder, her arm touching his hair.

"Still my lady?"

"Still your lady. Still my man?

"More than ever."

They lay still, passing into the realm where no words are necessary, a place where a touch sums up the years together. They clung to one another, then came apart, and in the silence of afterward let their interlaced fingers hold them together. Marie watched the side of her husband's face, seeing there that something was troubling him, something that he was turning 'round in his mind, looking at it from every side. She let the minutes slip past, ran her hand slowly through his hair, then asked,

"Is somethin' on yer mind?"

His eyes turned to her, and he managed a small smile.

"An operation. We got a tip on somethin' the Brits were supposed to be up to." He stopped speaking and pulled himself up to a sitting position, reworking the pillow until it suited him then continued.

"We checked a place out. Real discreet like. But it was strange. The whole time I had a feelin', a feelin' like we was the ones bein' watched. Like they was waitin' for us to step into a noose." Reaching over to the little table by the bed he struck a match, lit a cigarette, took a long inhalation then spoke.

"It was just a feelin'. I didn't say nothin'. But it was like I could almost smell the bastards. Like they was right there. I never had a feelin' like it before. Felt like they was right on top of us."

Marie took the cigarette from his hand, had a drag then handed it back as Louis added,

"I could almost feel 'em startin' to drool over what was strollin' into their little cookin' pot."

Marie felt a chill like something brushing past and she said, "Jesus Christ, Louis."

Her husband tilted his head back, pulling one knee up and resting his cigarette hand on it.

"Was awful odd, that feelin', couldn't shake it. An' no rational reason for it. Nothin' was outta place, nothin' unusual. Just the hair on the back a' me neck standin' up. Almost shiverin' I was, an' the sun beaten' down the whole time."

His wife wrapped her arms around herself.

"God, Louis. It's a warnin', so it is. It's yer guardian angel warnin' ya. Be careful a' that place whatever it is. Take heed, that's a warnin' plain an' simple. There's somethin' evil there, so there is."

Putting his cigarette out with several quick dabs he suddenly turned to kiss her neck,

"Think it's vampires?" he asked.

The woman crossed herself.

"Don't even be jokin' about that! Vampires. Christ, don't even say it. It frightens me awful, so it does." She nudged him. "Give me a cigarette then."

He lit the cigarette for her, then held it up to her mouth. Marie took in the butt's offerings, then exhaled.

"Don't be coddin' about vampires. It terrifies me, so it does."

He let the matter of the undead drop, as his wife gripped her cigarette, taking one rapid puff after another. He slid closer, giving her a long hug.

"Well, I'll listen to that guardian angel. We'll be handlin' that place real gentle like."

Pulling the cigarette away from her lips, Marie whispered.

"Good. That's good then."

Announced by the wind thudding against the windows, a shower blew in from the west, then seeking other games, it passed on. In its place came a cool dampness that settled on darkened streets and through open windows, probing worn floors and tugging at sheets.

His wife slept soundly, unmoving as the cool air sought new territory, claiming its right to be. Louis remained leaning back against the headboard of his married life.

The enemy had been there, he knew it. Knew it but could do no more than think it. If he spoke it he would spread weakness through his part of the movement. But he knew it. And what could he do? For he knew something else as surely as he knew his name. They would get him. Some how, some way, they would find him. And their English walls would close upon him, maybe forever. So there was no choice. He would stand, not bow. He would stand and face them, defy them.

Once as a child his family had gone to the beach. He had been shocked by the coldness of the water. At its relentless march inward with the turning of the tide. He had stood unmoving on the sand, facing each cold wave that smacked him.

Beneath his feet the water dug away the sand. And at last the sea had knocked him down. Louis smiled in the dark at how much he still loved that boy standing in the waves.

They were both staggering beneath the weight of all that was unsaid. She decided to put an end to their verbal waltz. Michaela spoke.

"Jimmy, listen. We can't stay here. We can't. Someone will find out, they always do. We have to go away, far away, and we have to do it quick."

"I won't run away. I won't leave my comrades."

She took a long drag of her cigarette then blew the smoke slowly out, letting it drift back against her face and over both shoulders.

"Comrades? Christ in heaven, they'd kill us both in a heartbeat. They wouldn't hesitate."

"Louis wouldn't."

She drew a breath for a retort but held her words, then sought wisdom in a long draw on the butt.

"No, he wouldn't."

He turned with a baleful look, took a drag on his own cigarette then turned his gaze over the rooftops toward the downtown. She watched him, thinking, *funny how when we're stuck we all look at them tall glass buildings. Like the answer is somehow inside them, locked in an office or room, as if there's some code for us in the neon, if only we could figure it out.* She reached out and touched his arm.

"Jimmy, I'll stand by you no matter what. But honest to God I'm scared. Scared for you an' for me. I know your secret. We're no different to them. Think ya can reason with 'em? Ya know better. They'll give some ones of 'em the job and that's it. Me an' you Jimmy. Two bodies in an empty lot an' no one knows nothin'. I want to live my life with you Jimmy. Not die next week with no one mournin' either one of us."

He didn't move, seemed not even to have heard her. But she knew him well enough to see the feelings he struggled with.

"Jimmy."

When he didn't look at her she reached out to squeeze his shoulder.

"Jimmy you've done enough. You've done your share an' more. No one can deny what you've done for Ireland, for her people. Jimmy, yer not Superman so you aren't. They tortured you, Jimmy. Christ almighty, yer only a human being. You've done enough. Come away with me. We can go to America, to Canada, we just have to go. We have to leave this place."

They both smoked, letting the comfort of it in and out. The smoke twisted and dissolved all around them. At length she dropped her cigarette, twisting it underfoot.

"Jimmy there's another thing. That copper knows. Do ya think he's above turning you in when it suits him?" Now for the first time her voice rose, as emotion spilled into her words.

"You're nothin' to any of 'em Jimmy. Nothin'. But yer everything there is to me."

When he turned he seemed to have shrunk inside his clothes and his voice wavered.

"I've never spent a night outside Belfast in my life. Never. What would I do? I wouldn't know where anything is."

Despite everything that had befallen her, she smiled.

"Things are where they're supposed to be. You'll find them. You'll be fine."

He flashed a look at her, fear dancing at the corners of it. It was the fear of a man who feels the ground sliding beneath him. She realized he didn't fear anything here. It was the peaceful places that frightened him. Those places and how a man like himself would find his worth in them. A man so long on a sharp edge that the rounded ways of routine terrified him.

Watching him, Michaela used her gift of seeing things in their simplest form. He saw this as the end of something. She saw it as a beginning of something. She only had to make him see what she saw. It was simple. She knew she could do it.

Leaning close she raised herself on tip toes and kissed his face. He smiled and she thought, *There, we've taken a first step together. Next we will walk along together. Then holding hands, we will leave this place. Leave it like two lovers emerging from a lake. The water will close behind us and all will be as before. A lake doesn't know when someone enters or leaves, and what does the water care?*

The warm orange glow of the cigarette caressing his fingers led the way, bouncing left and right, sniffing for the trail ahead. Jimmy followed, hugging the damp blackened walls of the Lower Falls, inhaling peat smoke, feeling nameless taut things within himself go slack.

He understood that he and Michaela could go away. Could be together somewhere in peace, a new beginning. *Wasn't that redemption? Wasn't it Jesus himself who said all could be forgiven? If. If the sinner had true remorse. Dear Jesus, I do have true remorse. I am heartily sorry. As a boy I drank in their songs, I stepped forward to enlist. I was vain, I was cruel, and I betrayed. No more Jesus, I only want to love her.*

You see my soul Lord, you know my every weakness, let me be with her. I will no longer betray, no longer inform. I will no longer seek and kill.

God, I'm lost. God help me, speak to me. The sisters taught us that the last trick of Satan was despair. God I despair in this place, this hell I volunteered for. His tears welled, not enough to fall, just enough to wipe with one sleeve. Again he drew on the cigarette, seeking the flavor his emotions had drained.

Certainty came with this exhalation of dry smoke. He would do it. He would go with her and start everything anew. He dropped the cigarette, stepped on it and listened to the neighborhood. Sometimes at night the place seemed to creak and groan with anxiety. Tonight, however, there was only the dark and the soft interrogative woof of a dog.

The woman was pointing to a path ahead and he would

walk that trail. He would take up the tools and tasks of an ordinary man. No more would he wear the face of vengeance, no longer be a man turned inside out. He would stand alone and beg God's forgiveness, then word by word he would strip off the uniform of his country's poetry.

The grass, trees and shrubs seemed to lunge at him, flashing staccato hellos and goodbyes simultaneously, making Jimmy a shivering and frightened pilgrim on an angry green ocean. The car hit the sharp rises of the country road like a stone skipping on a watery surface, Jimmy in a sweaty chill, a stomach-tightening dizziness. His gut squeezed ever tighter, pressing upward, the queasiness coming with it, wringing sweat from his brow as the copper yammered at him and the land rose and fell away.

MacDonald's face seemed to explode in size, leering at him like something in a cartoon as the copper screamed,

"Four fucking bombs! Four fucking bombs and you don't know a fucking thing? You think I was born yesterday, you lying bastard?"

"I'm not lying!"

"Shut up!"

A truck flashed over a rise, blasting its horn at the car that had drifted onto to its side of the road. MacDonald veered back across the center line, shaken, his train of thought blasted apart by the air horn thudding past.

The two men exchanged a quick look, not speaking, but each reflecting on the fact they had nearly been killed, and then each seeing the irony of being found dead together.

"Jesus," said Jimmy.

MacDonald glared at him then quickly turned to the road, addressing his words toward the twisting rural lane. Here the road sunk beneath surrounding pastures, the path so old it had worn its way into the earth. Then it would burst back up, teasing them with a glimpse of sky and country, a false promise that it would let a stranger know where he was. Jimmy leaned forward, steadying himself on the dash with one palm.

"It happened all at once. He didn't tell anyone in our group. The bombs were assembled, the cars were there, and the team called. Just like that. And he said no one was to leave. No one. It was assembled that fast."

MacDonald glanced at his passenger, then slowed just a bit. With the passing moments, the encounter with the truck was digging deeper into his psyche.

"Just like that, eh?"

"It was done an' done. There was nothin' to do but go along for the ride."

A village flowed past on both sides of them, a pub beckoned, the Rat and Parrot. He liked that name, he wished they could stop and have a good solid pint or two.

"And one van for the lot of you to get away?"

"Just the one. A regular bus, so it was."

MacDonald almost smiled as he squinted ahead.

"That would have been a nice day's work for our boys, if you'd run into a checkpoint."

"We were to stop peaceful like, then kill them all. No witnesses," Jimmy said.

He inwardly shouted with glee at the look that jumped onto the copper's face. Like a spider had stepped from his white Loyalist starched collar to his thick copper's neck. He was wide-eyed. Jimmy gave the information his own little twist.

"That was part of the plan," he continued. "The nine of us jumping out at once, guns blazing. 'Take the game right to 'em.' Louis's exact words. 'Take the game right to 'em.'"

Another look from the detective. *Not so cocky this time, are ye?* thought Jimmy. *Not so cocky at all, ya soulless bastard.*

Jimmy could see the man's mind working something else.

Figuring how to explain that a van with his confidential informant inside stopped at one of a hundred routine checkpoints around the city. Then it turned into an IRA clown car spewing out holy hell and death on half a dozen unsuspecting police officers.

The pair glanced at one another but both knew better than to speak. The road swept downward, its view opening onto the ocean, then it reversed, moving back among the greenery of the countryside, picking up villages, then towns as it made its way back to the city. At length Jimmy found his bearings, began to understand where they were. The copper stopped at a traffic light and turned to him.

"No more after-action reports, lad. No more 'we done this, we done that.' I want to know ahead of time. You figure out how you're going to do that. And you find out how those bombs got delivered to that wee team of yours. Find out and tell me."

"I understand."

This time Jimmy grabbed the money from the copper's hand and jumped out of the car, striding away with the envelope crushed in his grip.

MacDonald watched him go, drilling hate into the small of his back until he was a dot in the distance. Then the detective put the car in gear and moved into the traffic flow.

Pretending he was helping with the plan to escape, Jimmy let Michaela pretend she was following his lead. She spoke of train schedules, bus routes, a flat in Dublin, then she told him of small towns, places where she could be a waitress and he could find odd jobs.

As she spoke of the peace of the place they were headed to, he felt he was being dragged to the edge of a cliff. He could only hold her and try to smother his unformed fears, the knowledge coming into focus that he had to kill the man he was and become someone others expected to see. This new man must love his work, his hammer and saw, the beer lorry arriving in the morning at his little pub, the dry scratching of his broom upon the public way.

And he was to love this woman who loved the man who was to be no more. He was to love her and not look back, was to exchange her tender caress for the slap on the arm and intimate insults of his comrades. He was to stand in her unwavering, unquestioning admiration and turn away from the respect of men that had to be earned every day. He was to deny the sacred past and live among those whose patriotism consisted of manufactured tunes and tears dripping into pints of stout. He was to keep his mouth shut.

And he did.

In Dublin he reported for day labor jobs where he carried bricks up ladders, rolled kegs of beer early in the morning past rows of frantic pedestrians migrating to offices and counters. He stood in a deep hole shoveling while five others leaned on tools staring down. Then he looked into the earth as one of the others labored, no one speaking, all thinking of cold beer and passing girls. Then home from that, climbing the stairs to the rented flat, too tired to love her, too alone to go out for a pint.

In three weeks they had some money and were off to the west near Roscommon with its rain smoothed hills and its ten thousand small town secrets, its litany of slights.

With darkness, they loved. There was no one and nothing else but the other in twisting embrace. This passion promised deliverance, promised reasons why, assured them of something eternal. It was all there in that space between fingertips and the lover, if only they could possess it, if only they could embrace deeply enough, hold tight enough, share the same breaths, same gaze, same heat, then they would have it.

In the morning they awoke intertwined, with the pillows on the floor, the sheets twisted even whiter. Then they found their lovemaking was only lovemaking, as dawn tapped its fingers, impatient to be let in, trailing behind it the ever heavier day demanding to be lived.

Day came to her framed by her love for him. Everything came through the prism of that emotion and everything bent its light to her reality. But for Jimmy the days brought the faces of Belfast, the accusations of the dead shouting through shattered skulls, the slow steps of hunters shifting through everything he had ever touched.

The air grew tight around him, like he was in one of those chambers they put the deep sea divers in. Surely the compressed air would shatter his hearing then press his eyes to blindness. There the northern men would find him, sightless in the bright sun, and he wouldn't even know they were approaching, would not hear their soft footfalls until they pressed cold metal to his temple.

He kept all that wrapped inside, covered over by the deep fiber of scars. This is what pulsed now and then, letting him know it was there, telling him all he presented to the world was standing on the wet sand of the spirit he'd traded away. He longed to understand this man he was to become, while yearning for the secret to make him go away.

Jimmy folded and refolded the empty paper, pin pricks of sweat coming to life on the back of his hands, chasing words but stirring only muffled sounds and sharp features. At length he understood there was no explanation, there was only the need to tell what he had done and what he was about to do. There was everything that had been between himself and Louis, and now there was only betrayal. When he realized that, he could trace the sentences, could tell all that had happened without asking for forgiveness, understanding, or mercy. He knew now how simple it all was, and he wrote simply. Then he signed his name.

He stared at the inadequate signature and saw the last logical conclusion, the last split from the numbers of comrades. Divided like their country, again and again and again, right to the separating of himself and Louis. The parting unto death of the one and only friend he had ever had. Running a finger over the phrase, he sealed the envelope and turned to Michaela, who stood at a respectful distance. She watched him send the letter on its way, then they crossed the lobby of the city's central post office and walked down Dublin's Connolly Street.

When they had taken seats on the local bus she saw in his glance his cry for silence.

Michaela thought, *If only I could make him understand, if only he could see the future, little children and security, a home, the love of all those around.* She knew he could not see that but he could see her. And if he saw her clearly he would see all that she brought to him. It was all within her, their future was within her heart, their children were there, their new home as well, it was all there and she could raise her hand and feel the contours of their new life.

But he could not. He was afraid, confused. Unlike hers, his heart was ripped in two different directions and he couldn't see or feel anything but that rending.

But he would feel the new, she was positive he would. He would see the future, hear and see the world beyond his streets and the surrounding forest of wet walls. In that forest he kept questioning who he was, what he had done and become. The fate she saw would, with her love, allow her to take his hand and lead him from his wilderness of mirrors.

"Hey."

He started at her voice. She leaned over, gesturing him closer, to come within earshot of her whisper.

"I love you."

He mouthed the same words and she leaned back, smiling at him. *There* she thought, *there my love, see you have taken a step, now hold my hand and take another.*

The damp night followed Louis Duffy as he entered his home, spilling around his feet, spreading into the silence of the empty dwelling. The man of the house was looking forward to some solitude from the tumult of wife and kids that their visit to Marie's sister provided.

Louis prowled the kitchen looking for a snack, found rolls and butter, a kettle waiting to be heated and tea by the sink. He was a happy man as he stood near the stove digging a wide knife into soft butter. Whistling a tune, he turned on the stove and measured the tea, then got a cup and a small plate. His melody ended when soft roll met lips and then the kettle took up a song of its own. Balancing plate, cup and food, he entered the living room setting his burden on the arm of his chair, then switched on the television.

He emitted a small breath of surprise at the letter addressed to him that Marie had set atop the TV. Louis usually got two birthday cards each year from the same two relatives. At Christmas his name was added as a courtesy to the deluge of cards his wife sent and received. Easing back into his chair he lifted the envelope that lacked any return address, seeing something familiar in the handwriting but not able to place it.

With the letter balanced on a knee he took a bite of the buttered roll and a long sip of tea. Then putting the food and drink back on their perch, he carefully opened the missive.

No one was there to see the ruddy cheer and health drain from his cheeks, no one heard the whispered *Jesus Christ*. No one returned the wide-eyed stare. In that chair Louis felt his heartbeat, felt his insides turn like the gentle tumbler of a huge safe, a safe with a heavy door that was sliding, sliding to lock him inside, leaving him a shrinking pathway of light to run through.

Louis saw everything at once, as though a mural was suddenly hanging before him in mid-air. He saw a broken friend, the raid that took Big Mick and the others, Jimmy's questions about the sniper, the thousand hesitancies and downcast glances he had attributed to British brutality and now saw to be stark Irish betrayal.

Even as he went through the front door to run to his wife and warn her, the mural added another scene, one with himself in it. He had told Jimmy there was a woman working for them inside Royal Avenue barracks. *Jesus, they'd get her sure as the sun shone, get her and everything and everyone the girl had ever touched. And they'd reserve a special fury for her having played them for the fools.*

He couldn't bear that image, and as he ran he pushed it away, shoved it to that place where all the horrors dwelt, shoved it down an alley so it could bob to the surface on some other street.

A few doors down from where his wife was he stopped, knowing that the less she knew the better for her, realized that his being calm was best for the family. At the door she saw right through his façade, knew better to question when he said he had to go away for a bit, managed not to cry when he hugged his children, then he vanished into the night.

Her sister understood as well, and when his figure disappeared into the gloom of the Lower Falls, the two women told the children to stay by the telly. Then they went into the little kitchen to fall into one another's arms, holding in their sobs so as not to frighten the wee ones.

Something awoke Laurie Drumlin, something like a door slamming and running feet. She listened, turning her head left then right, each movement bringing pain, the bare light bulb on the ceiling unblinking in its mockery.

The blood in her nostrils had congealed, no longer adding to the darkening of the front of her paper smock. Other crimson droplets were finding their way into her throat, she felt them move but they had no taste.

Slumped in the corner of the room, she shifted her weight to lean on the wall behind her.

The headache stabbed anew, like a spike right in the top of her head and with the back of her left hand she felt the new terrain of her face. The lumps, the closed left eye, the lips swollen like slices of foam rubber.

The pummeling had changed her face, battered and broken it and then denied her the relief of seeing what they had done. But Laurie knew she had heard a door slam and footsteps on pavement, and the longer she listened the more clearly she understood the sounds had come from within her, had entered her mind silently and took form only when safely within. Someone was trying to tell her something, she knew it. Someone was running away and thinking of her. She was not alone.

When the beastly women came again to her cell she would look right at them and spit. She could do that, it wasn't much. But she could do it and let them kill her then. She'd told them nothing and they were getting angrier, meaner, the female in them becoming raw and basic, jealous and sharp-clawed. Laurie saw that, and saw that for now she was winning. And she saw men moving on rainy sidewalks and they were thinking of her and that was all she needed.

Holy Mary mother of God, now and at the hour of our death, amen.

Now the footsteps were not running, not ethereal, they were as real as the big key on its wide metal ring probing her door. As real as the institutional smell of the soap these women bathed in, as real as the pain radiating from the clump of blonde hair one grabbed, real as the slaps jumping from their pudgy pale hands.

Louis stepped into a tall narrow wooden doorway, watching the glowing arcs of cigarettes at a corner far up the street. He removed his jacket, letting the cool air work over him, cool him and calm his breathing. Then he stepped onto the sidewalk, striding up the middle of the street, making the red tips of the butts pause, seeing one of them drop to the pavement at his approach. The boys were local and he nodded at them.

"Ye know me?" he inquired.

"Aye,"

He gave them five names.

"Find them. No matter what they're doin', tell them to come here straight away."

The boys scattered as Louis thought of the girl on the inside. He didn't know where she lived, just what she provided. He would have to send word up the chain to reach her and tell her to run.

A figure appeared from around the corner, Black Peter Riordan, the driver, walking as fast as he dared, his ebony hair in train behind, as in the distance another figure strode into view and in minutes they were all gathered. Silent as friars at vespers they stood waiting for Louis to speak.

"We've been betrayed," Louis told them.

As he explained he could see an occasional grimace in the

dark, hear the sucking sounds of lips parted by shock, could almost touch the low curses as he told the men to scatter. To avoid the usual places and to keep moving. In three days they would communicate.

"Think now lads, where you'll be. Think and tell no one but myself."

He stood apart from them momentarily, then beckoned them one by one to tell the place where a message to meet could be sent. And one by one they were gone, most walking, one breaking into a run, racing to kiss goodbye infant and pregnant wife.

Then Louis was alone with just his fear and fury, imagining himself screaming at Jimmy, shaking him. But he could not see guns or bullets, wrist ties, or a hood. Others could see that and demand everything. Louis only wanted to ask why, even though he knew what the reply would be.

I don't know.

Ian MacDonald glanced at his telephone with the feeling of a traveler glancing down the track for his train. The ring of the phone, like the train bending into sight, would bring movement, energy, and perhaps, the pleasure of the new. For when that device emitted its call information would pour forth. Information from a little bitch who had wormed her way into the body of the security apparatus to kill that very body. She was a parasite, and there was only one way to deal with such an organism. Destroy it. Kill it, and everything it had come in contact with. And Ian MacDonald was just the man for the task.

In his little home office the detective slid his chair away from the desk and its mundane minutiae of merciless combat. He stretched, putting both hands behind his neck, feeling the gentle pull of the muscles of his lower back.

Dropping his arms, he emitted a soft sigh. Again looking at the telephone, he had to fight the urge to pick it up and dial his MI5 contact. Just to see how things were going with the lovely little jewel he had presented them. But he didn't dial. That would be bad form, might seem as though he was unhappy with the pace of things, unhappy or unprofessional. If they had something to report they would let him know. And when they did he would be there to look at the shocked expressions as he pulled the bastards from their beds, hit their safe houses, their arms depots and their so-called social clubs. He loved this feeling, this aching delay, like reaching to unbutton the blouse of a willing woman.

Only one matter prevented everything from being perfect.

Jimmy had missed his appointed time to check in. It was the first time he had done so. MacDonald had half a mind to have the little shit arrested and roughed up. But he'd give the lad a chance this one time. Perhaps he had simply forgotten, or maybe he was just being stubborn. It was just like them to dig in their heels when they came up with some tidbit. And the girl was quite the little tidbit indeed.

He'd contact Mister Jimmy Fitzgerald tomorrow and set him straight, maybe have the girlfriend lifted as well. See how the little weasel liked that. Let the boy know who was running this particular show.

Louis walked with his fingertips brushing the walls of houses and storefronts. His mind presented him a map of the area and he could see the homes of friends and relatives on that map. As he focused he saw distant relatives, heard friends from long ago. Boys he'd played football with, the parents of girls he'd gone to school with, the distant cousins of cousins he hardly knew. These people would be his lifeboat, he would drift on the waters of nodding acquaintances right under the Brits' noses.

They could not trace him. There was only the chance that a random raid would fall upon him. But every raid caused a counter punch of rocks, bottles and abuse. Nothing brought the cause to life like British troopers smashing in the doors and windows of Irish homes. Let them come. The harder they hit, the more recruits would be lined up for the cause. Let them exhaust themselves banging against the rocks of Irish nationalism. Let the bastards come.

His knock was gentle, as soft as the link of second cousins by marriage, the door was opened slowly and the man who opened it whispered Louis's name in surprise.

"I'm needin' a place to stay for a bit," said Louis.

The man nodded and Louis stepped forward, the door closing behind him as gently as it had opened.

Short grouchy William T. Flaherty carried the burdens of existence on his freckled bald head. He had only the one girl on duty today because Michaela had not shown up, had not called, had sent no explanation. His inquiry about Michaela to her friend Liz Moran had produced only a rush of fear in that girl, fear that, Flaherty knew, could blossom into feeling ill and needing to go home.

So the shop man let the subject alone and went about his path of chores. He unctuously added numbers on a yellow sheet of paper as Liz stood behind the cash register. That was what they were doing when the bell above the door clanged, the door slammed off the wall, and three strange men entered. One of them flipped the small sign listing the stores hours.

"You're closed," he said.

"Closed?" sputtered Flaherty.

"Shut up," said the man.

Like the other two he was in his late twenties, wore jeans, a long sleeved sweatshirt. He grabbed Flaherty like he was a package to be delivered and pulled him into the back room as the other two pointed Liz Moran into a small pantry in the opposite corner.

Liz froze and her lips moved uncontrollably. The men just glared at her as she began to shake, felt the strength leaving her knees, reached out to the wall that guided her as she slid down to the floor weeping.

"Shut up," said the younger of the two guards, which made her dissolve in soft choking sounds that formed a backdrop to

Flaherty's pleading in the back room. The only other sounds were the occasional tugs on the front door by customers who were unable to believe that Flaherty, who was said to still possess the first quid he ever made, had closed.

A housewife pressed her face to the door, then a teenager out to buy cigarettes kicked the door in frustration. Moments later that sound was answered by the thump of Flaherty hitting the floor after being smacked on the temple with the butt of a .357 magnum. The leader who had struck him strode out, grabbed Liz Moran by the arm and led her to the room next to the crumpled and moaning man. He was calm the way some men get when they are very angry.

"Where is Michaela?"

"I swear to God I don't know."

"Where's Jimmy?"

"I've no idea. I swear. I don't know where they are. She's my friend an' I'm worried sick about her, so I am. But I don't know where she is. Or him either."

He pulled the gun from his belt, holding it with his elbow bent, the weapon pointed at the ceiling.

"One lie an' yer dead," he declared.

He demanded she tell him about the relationship of Jimmy and Michaela, of their plans, their dreams, their walks and meetings. He demanded everything and she answered all of it as the man on the floor lay still. She saw the blood squeezing through the fingers of the hand he pressed to his head, she even heard another tug on the front door.

Liz Moran talked, hardly knowing what she was saying, and she talked and talked and couldn't stop. She giggled, she wept and she watched the red liquid slowly find a path to Flaherty's elbow.

Then the three men pulled the captives to their feet, and led them back to the cash register and the worn counter with the yellow accounting sheet.

"We weren't here," said the leader before turning for the door.

The youngest of them stopped at the sign, flipped it, then declared,

"Yer open."

Ian MacDonald settled in at his desk, turning the page of his small calendar, checking that his ballpoint pens were arranged properly, monitoring the tides of this place, the currents set in motion by information gleaned, denied, and inferred.

He checked his messages, for there was a strict protocol if a confidential informant missed a call-in. The informant was to check in first thing the next morning. Failing that, he was to call in at noon. If that call did not take place the turned man was to contact the detective as soon as he was able.

People who walked the high wire seldom forgot the consequence of a misstep. And, the policeman knew, most grew addicted to their cash gifts, their free meals at out of the way restaurants and in darkened automobiles. Most came to almost demand these tiny perquisites because they were components of the new persona the detective had created.

MacDonald had broken informants and formed them, had all but renamed them. He liked to believe that each had a bit of himself inside, making him especially attuned to their pride, shame and vagaries. Now, that sensitivity to a particular informant was causing the first real quiver of alarm within the special branch officer. Jimmy Fitzgerald never forgot what he had become or what he was expected to do. It was gnawing at him every second he drew breath.

Touching the tips of his multi-colored pens, the detective knew something had happened. MacDonald saw three possibilities. Jimmy was lying very ill in hospital, Jimmy had been found out by the IRA, or Jimmy was hiding. The detective picked up his phone and dialed area hospitals, asking if one James M. Fitzgerald was among their patients. The replies came back that he was not.

The policeman drummed the fingers of his right hand on the desktop, musing about the remaining two possibilities. Jimmy was hiding or Jimmy was revealed. His left hand came up to the desk to tap-tap along with its mate. Looking down at his hands, MacDonald saw an option in each. Move quickly and try to minimize the damage, or move slowly so as not to tip the other side that the security forces were in motion.

A quick move would not likely catch the wayward rat, a slow move might draw him toward the light. But if the IRA had Jimmy, slow movement would be precious information gained by the enemy. Examining the tip of a newly sharpened pencil, the detective reached a Belfast decision. Hit hard. Hit fast.

Trouble shouted its greetings over the rooftops of Leeson Street, growling its arrival with the engines of a dozen armored cars. Before the machines came into view children had been rushed inside, young men vanished from street corners and old women hurried mops and brooms from sidewalk to closet. The drum roll of these engines was prelude to what exploded on the neighborhood as a full company of paratroopers burst from the vehicles and into the lore of dozens of families.

Michaela's flat was hit, Louis's front door knocked off its hinges, the Long Bar was grabbed and slapped like a cheating girlfriend, Big Mick's house was hit, his widow screaming punching and spitting at the intruders. Any male of military age caught outside was grabbed and beaten.

The mid-day sippers at the Cracked Cup were shoved like flailing fish into one corner and pounded with truncheons. However, these men erupted back at their tormentors. Bar stools flew, bottles hit the Paras, as did fists and feet. British reinforcements poured through the door and the battle turned. Hauled face down toward the armored cars, they would face the next level of abuse. But these local habitués had earned the right to repeat a local mantra. *One Irishman arrested makes more noise than six million Jews.*

Only at Flaherty's store did the men in maroon berets pull up in their assault. One look at Liz Moran and Flaherty told the princes of mayhem they were not blazing their usual virgin trail, but following in someone's footsteps. It was that indignant message that crackled up the chain of command, and brought Liz and the shopman to the detective's place of business.

Upon arrival, the pair was in opposite emotional trajectories. The man was barely in control of the muscles that moved him. Strolling his little beach of routine, he had been knocked off his feet by the bone numbing wave of the guerrillas. Now he was about to be thrown against the jagged reef of the coppers. William T. Flaherty wanted only to crawl up the warm sands and hide.

The woman, who ordinarily would be terrified by the sight of a spider, had locked onto a knot of righteous indignation and loyalty to her best friend. She was getting angrier by the minute, finding within herself the ancient rage of her people and the furious wisdom that you can't lose because you have nothing to lose.

Seeing all this in a glance, MacDonald gestured for them to be put in opposite soundproof cells. Then he told the squad of Paras they'd done good work, offering them a bit of tea. The raiders received this gesture with the shy gratitude of boys complimented by a schoolmarm.

Almost managing a smile at the sight, Detective MacDonald strode down the corridor to the door behind which William T. Flaherty cringed in muffled horror, all his thoughts bouncing off the soundproofing on the walls and off the ceiling with its bare bulb whispering doom.

Ian MacDonald let himself into the room, drawing a gasp of fright from the man in the corner. The detective believed in husbanding his resources, his energy, his words, and he didn't want to waste any of those things on this little man who might hold big information. He crouched over the table his knuckles pressed white, like a footballer ready to lunge.

"There are paratroopers outside ready to attach battery cables to your balls. Understand?"

"Yes, Sir."

"Be the least bit dishonest with me and I'll call them."

"Yes, Sir."

"Tell me where Jimmy Fitzgerald is and where Michaela is. Then tell me everything you know about each of them."

And Flaherty did. He spoke and spoke, he giggled and sweated, he wiped the suddenly appearing saliva from his lips and chin. Then he talked some more, and MacDonald saw the man was being quite honest. So without so much as a nod, the cop stood and went out the door, leaving Flaherty hanging by the threads of his fear.

Three doors down MacDonald found a woman standing with her back to a corner of the room.

"Where's Michaela?"

"Go to hell."

"Don't make it hard for yourself."

"Go to bloody hell and burn."

The policeman and the shop girl stared at one another across centuries of religion, loyalties, class and gender. The girl's breaths were hot and sharp, the man's slow and measured. Then MacDonald closed the door gently behind him and walked back to his office.

Again checking that his pens and pencils were properly aligned, he took a single piece of lined yellow stationery and drew the outlines of a plan. His prize informant was neither ill in hospital nor in the hands of the IRA, who the detective now understood wanted Jimmy as badly as he did. So his prize and his prize's lover had run off. MacDonald slowly traced one word with a pencil. *Where?*

MacDonald thought of an article he'd read about shopping carts in America. So many had been stolen from store car lots that American businessmen had installed little electronic devices in them. When they reached the edge of the lot their wheels stopped turning. Jimmy was the cart and Belfast was the lot. Jimmy couldn't move out of Belfast, couldn't imagine it. But the woman could. She could carry that boy anywhere. All she had to do was keep both hands on the wheel and keep going forward. The woman was the deck's wild card and she'd stolen the policeman's joker.

Ian MacDonald was infuriated and professionally embarrassed. And though he closed his eyes when the realization flashed within him, he was also more than a little jealous.

Leaning back, his wide chair emitting little squeaks, the detective rocked slowly. He tasted all the emotions this jealousy brought, he let them simmer and grow warmer. And he planned. Who to bring in and try to break, who to let swim free in the hope of them leading to others.

Today, he decided, was a day to tidy up. To straighten lines and connect dots. Underlings could mete out punishment and fear. He would have them check the bus and train stations, the haunts and secondary hangouts. He would rest today. He would crouch by the stream and pan for gold nuggets. Tomorrow he would resume the chase in earnest, and he would run the bastards down.

Thomas Duffy, six years of age, traced his name in the sugar layered on the counter by the kitchen sink. Then he drew a face in the white substance, touched his finger to his lips and turned to take in his world torn inside out. The adults ignored him, the men busy putting chairs and lamps rightside-up, the women bustling all around, both his aunts muttering in anger, his Ma alone, brushing something from her eye as she again attacked the stains all along the kitchen walls.

At first the adults had held him, assured him and promised candy later on. Now they had all put him aside for their adult work, and he could feel his lips trembling as he took in what the soldiers had done to his home. He didn't want to cry in front of all these people but it seized him and he began to bawl. He wept for the ground that was no longer under him, for his Da vanished in the night, for his favorite sweets now mashed with dirt, and he cried because he felt all alone.

His outburst stopped the grown-ups, the women sighing, the men seeming embarrassed. His mother moved quickly, shooing him into the parlor where ripped cushions spread their innards on the thin rug, where the television screen was a black open wound. Taking him by the arm Marie Duffy gave him one firm shake and demanded,

"Who was it put yer grandpa in prison?"

The boy hesitated and she squeezed his arms again, insisting,

"Who?"

"The Brits."

"Aye," said his mother.

"Who wants to get yer Da an' lock him away?"

"The Brits."

"Aye," said the woman, smoothing his hair.

"An' tell me, Thomas Duffy, who done this to ye today?"

"The Brits."

"Who?"

This time he spoke louder.

"The Brits."

She came down on both knees.

"Why did they do this to ye?"

"Because I'm Irish."

"Correct. Tell me again what ya are."

"I'm Irish."

"An' who is it hates the Irish, who is it robs the Irish, who is it murders the Irish?"

"The Brits."

She took his head in both her hands to whisper.

"An' who will protect yer mother from the Brits when he's a strong man?"

"I will."

"Why?"

"Because I'm Irish."

She pressed his cheeks with both her hands.

"There's my wee man then. A brave Belfast boy, tough an' strong, fearin' no one. Now get out an' help the men with the furniture."

With those words she kissed him on both cheeks and the trembling left him, the fear as well, replaced by the excitement of working with the men, and the pride of who and what he was. Then Thomas Duffy went to help the men to right the bureau and ponder along with them how to balance it now that it had but three legs.

Flaherty had become a child's hole in a sandy beach. Now and then a little bit more of him caved into the hole, and each breeze brushed hot dry sand onto its moist center. In his soul Flaherty had already run, already offered up the business, his name, his family, already piled all of it on the sidewalk outside the store and atop the mound had placed his manhood and a sign reading, *FREE*. His family would take the anger, the blame, absorb rising and plunging emotions he sucked from the bottle. And finally as men like him do, he would fall into self pity.

Then, without confrontation or the smallest accusation, he would flee. His wife and children would be dragged behind, a loose string of cheap baubles, scraping the pavement and the dirt. Part of them would break off and roll to the gutters, part would be picked up and tossed by strangers, part would cling to what was dragging them, coming to rest in his pool of shame and rage. And there they would stay.

Moods flashed through Liz Moran the way pedestrians' faces flash past a speeding driver. This girl who never spoke ill of anyone had at first been terrified, then resigned, now seethed. Never one for emotional nuance, a girl who had always blurted her feelings before they fully formed in her mind, she was now mentally focused, calm, and thoughtful.

She had seen that the man who ran her working life was weak and defeated. Her best friend had vanished, and because of that the soldiers had come and wiped their foreign boots on Liz and everything she cared for.

Liz felt something new surging within her, like when she

had first become a young woman, but slower, deeper, more consuming, infinitely more certain. She looked at the unlit cigarette in her hand, and then glanced toward the end of the block where several lads stood. She knew who they were, they were the edge of the revolt. They were that layer that led to another. They were a doorway to another world, a world running parallel to this one but vibrating with the moment and the movement.

Liz Moran walked slowly down the sidewalk, the lads noting her, knowing she'd never more than nodded to them. She walked up to the oldest, the best looking of them. Without a word she put her cigarette to her lips and waited. He produced a match, and as he did so she held his wrist with both hands to steady the flame. Then she drew deeply from the cigarette, exhaled the smoke and looked into his eyes.

"Thanks," was all she said. That word turned a key, and she felt the door beginning to open, and she felt a calm she had never known before.

Ian MacDonald sat at his kitchen table, his wife's fingers digging into the day's tension that had settled in his neck and shoulders. Usually her touch would dissipate the knots beneath his flesh, the tight fists of pain that roosted there. But this discomfort was deeper. It was like she was tapping on the other side of a wall. He could hear her efforts but felt no relief.

Rounding up prisoners was an opportunity to cultivate knowledge. A word, an expression, something blurted in rage, something obstinately denied, it all set a pattern.

Now the detective thought he knew what had happened. Jimmy had not been found out. Jimmy and the girl had fled. No one knew where, and the IRA was after them both. So the IRA knew before the security forces knew. And Louis and his cutthroats had gone on the run, while putting out a death sentence on Jimmy.

What the hell had happened? The policeman reached up to take hold of both his wife's wrists, kissed one of them and said "Thanks." He would let the pain lie. Let it speak to him and make him sharper.

Sitting straight up, flexing his shoulders, he saw career trouble in every direction. They all operated in their career bubble within the larger mayhem of everything outside. His informant gone, an IRA commander he was monitoring on the run, information only dribbling back, like drops from an old faucet. But he'd hit their safe houses, grabbed a couple of their volunteers, some of their weapons and papers.

He pondered some more. This may not be as bad for his

career as it looked at first glance. For he had learned one fast rule in the business of bending and breaking rules. He hadn't written one goddamn thing down about Jimmy. So he might get a verbal reprimand, a few sharp looks, but as far as the great grinding security apparatus was concerned, none of this had happened.

Her keepers had become nervous at the approaching court appearance, clearing their throats and fidgeting with their uniforms. Laurie laughed at them and their having concern over how they looked in a secret court.

The two women had pinned Laurie's arms and forced the make-up to her face. First the base, then a brush of rouge here and there, their subject resisting every dab of color, every rub beneath her eyes until they called a third woman who got her in a headlock as they struggled to make her presentable. They even got some lipstick on her by jamming thumbs into both cheeks, making her feel like a fish in a tank as they swiped the too-red lipstick and whispered curses in both her ears.

It exhausted them, this task of trying to make more attractive a beautiful woman they hated. It drained their color, and one had sweat beneath her arms and above her lips as they walked the corridor, passed through a walled yard and up two flights of stairs and into the courtroom. A high ceiling proclaimed solemnity, a wigged judge tradition, as Laurie sat when told to stand. The women yanked her to her feet. She went limp in their arms, until the judge told them to sit her back down.

She did not look at the man the government sent to represent her when he announced that the accused refused to recognize the court. Laurie heard the words. Espionage, conspiracy, terrorist organization. She pushed the words away, sitting with eyes closed until they yanked her up again to hear her sentence. Thirty years.

Now bearing her away, her guards relaxed, bumping her

between them as they retraced their steps. She looked up at the sky as they went through the yard. In the corridor they increased their gait, down an echoing corridor then toward daylight again. A police van was backed to the stairs outside and her guards pushed her handcuffed arms higher behind her, bending her forward, making her stumble into the van.

But she heard the voices, heard the Irish accents chant her name.

The guards winced. Laurie smiled. She heard the commotion as the van pulled onto the street, heard the English and Irish voices shouting, heard something bang off the van as it accelerated.

They know, she thought, *they know*. That would be enough for today. That would carry her today. Tomorrow would bring what tomorrow would bring. She could get through today, those Irish voices would carry her forward, they would not leave her, not today, not any day.

Roscommon was an area of sheep markets, cattle, insular pubs, insular people, and a bus line to the outside world. Luck came with this place in the form of two job openings. One for Michaela in the afternoon at a local pub, one for Jimmy at a construction site, where his accent was immediately recognized, his reticence respected and his work acceptable.

He told them he was newly married, so they understood why he wasn't up for a pint after work. And they did not pry about what had caused him to leave Belfast, taking the far-awayness in his eyes explanation enough. The man, they told one another, had seen terrible things, and sure, didn't anyone deserve a rest from all of that?

Word came to them of the wife he had working at Hunt's Pub, of her beauty, the captivating eyes, and the smile for everyone she met. Then they thought all the more of the man, and they joked of how he had the energy to even show up to labor after a night with such a lovely young woman.

As for Michaela, those around her in the afternoon felt the glow of the love she held within, coming close to bask in that feeling, then falling back to remember, hope.

The newly arrived couple spent nights in a rented flat in the part of town where lanes open their arms to pastures, where the settled balances uneasily upon the untamed. Each night seemed to hold the promise of resolution, only to end with the dark staring into the eyes of a too-soon dawn.

Even surrounded by peace, Jimmy struggled to find a place to rest, something that would push back to tell him that all about him was firm. But he couldn't find it. Instead he twisted, his weight pressing him against this alien terrain, pushing ever harder to whisper he did not belong.

The woman saw this labor as his adjusting to a new freedom, a testing of the curved boundaries of her love for him. He felt it as something invisible come to surround him, to drag him down and smother him and carry him to the thin woods of the region.

She waited for him to see all that was possible, to understand that with her the world belonged to him and him alone. He waited for the weight to leave his chest, for the departure of the certainty that something was coming up from behind. And he waited for the silent movement of the back door latch when the night was in full cry, the clouds scudding near and only the ancient fields there to see.

In the light of each false dawn she stirred and began preparation for their day. He heard her, greeted her, touched her and rose. And they went their separate ways.

Without the greedy moon thousands of stars pressed tight to the sky's black canopy, insisting, waiting, teachers wielding the power of silence. The couple too hung in silence as they walked, hands entwined, occasionally squeezing a message of affection, giving the other a glance, not wanting to disturb, until Michaela spoke.

"You can sail by the stars."

Jimmy looked up quickly, taking in the night, then settled his gaze on Michaela. She took his arm by the elbow slowly pulling him around.

"Remember when we decided to leave? You said you wouldn't know where anything was. Remember?"

The dark hid his blush.

"I do."

"Well then."

She stopped, searching overhead for several seconds.

"OK."

Her right hand shot up.

"There see? It's the Starry Plough, what some call the Big Dipper. See it?"

He nodded.

"I do."

She pressed closer, taking his wrist and elbow to lift his arm and point it.

"All the stars are moving, all but one."

She pressed her face to his arm, lifting his index finger to aim.

"Polaris, the north star."

She told him to follow the last star in the plow, it pointed at Polaris.

"Polaris never moves. It's always to the north. It even tells you how many degrees from the equator you are. Look, it's about 52 degrees above the horizon. That's where we are, 52 degrees above the equator. South is behind us, west is left, east is right."

He grasped the lesson at once, saying, "So even if we were on the ocean we'd know where we were."

"Correct."

He stood, returning the gaze of the far away worlds.

"North."

Pausing he repeated,

"North."

Then he lifted both his arms to shoulder height. Turning his head right he said,

"East."

Turning left he said,

"West."

He looked at her,

"Fifty-two degrees."

"Aye."

"Brilliant."

"Now yer a navigator."

Again they walked in silence, the path taking them along the edge of the field then in a wide loop back toward their cottage.

As they strolled Jimmy glanced up, but the sky markers were lost amid a million unblinking brethren. Only Michaela's gentle voice broached the silence, and Jimmy was content to grasp her warm hand, feeling its contours, its magic, its extended fingers of belief.

Twin white candles danced before the mirror atop the walnut colored bureau, precariously balancing the gloom of drizzle outside. That light held the man and woman in balance as well, steadying them as they peered into the open promise of one another's eyes.

For a long time afterward he lay still, staring at the ceiling and its opaque montage of things almost known, people almost there, of answers just out of reach. Then his sureness began to seep away, and he felt like the mattress was rising, shooting higher and higher into the black night, and he waited for the empty-gut feeling of the rising's apex, it's inevitable bow to earth's pull. But it didn't come, and he floated ever higher into the night, twisting in the dark without direction, with nothing pulling him and nothing to push against.

Later, lying awake, he heard her breathe as he caressed those fingers one by one. Wanting all of their certainty while knowing he could never possess it. He understood he could appreciate it, see its results, its glow, its expressions, melody and tone. But he could not have it. Not for himself, not ever.

This woman's love brought me inside and now my face is pressed to the cold damp window looking out not in. But it is not enough. I love her, but what really is love to a man? Refuge, praise, understanding, the knowing of my moods, the answers to questions I didn't even know I was asking. Add all that up. Subtract who I am and what I've done. What you get is zero.

In the brief weeks they had been in this place, routine had found them. Today Michaela was home before Jimmy, and had time to prepare a meal. In early evening he would appear with his quick city walk, ears alert for all the missing sounds, looking left and right for traffic that wasn't there.

Always she paused to observe him, to embrace his movement, to love the strides erasing the distance between them. Now she waited for his appearance, tended to a simmering pot, looked through the window, adjusted a flame, waiting, watching, stirring the meal. Above, low white clouds filled the sky, holding among them raggedy blue patches as they hurried past, as though rushing the torn sky pieces off for mending.

The first doubt came to her like a whisper, to chill her and settle. Then that doubt found voice telling her:

He's gone back.

She shook her head *no*, watching as the clouds flowed, as they twisted ever so slightly to glance down and confirm. And she knew. Jimmy had returned to Belfast's red bricks and concrete. All she was, everything she had to give, was not enough. As far as she could reach, as tight as she could embrace, she had not held that secret part of him. She had not possessed the key to all within, had not seen the contents of those hidden rooms.

She didn't cry out or weep. She only held her love with none to share it, and that pain spread outward and came to draw her face tight, make her eyes dry, to draw simple lines where none had been.

Leaning against the wall of the small kitchen she could see what she felt, was able see its color, test its weight, its flavor, hear its voice. As she felt the numbing coolness grow within her, it was all as simple as a single word. Alone.

For company he had an unlit cigarette and the faces of all the drivers from Roscommon to Belfast. He had their jokes and grimaces, the air brakes and grinding gears, the worn phrases about The Troubles, the awfulness of it all, and the hurried goodbyes at crossroads and intersections.

Jimmy paused at the edge of his world, waited for the sun to go down so he could reenter everything he knew. In twilight he walked along the streets, each block growing more familiar, and now he was in this abandoned building in the heart of his land.

Again he twirled the cigarette through his fingers, contemplating the beauty of it, aching to devour it, knowing he could not because its glow, its fragrance, might draw curiosity. So he held the treasure wrapped in its white paper. Touching it with the fingertips of his free hand he recalled his first one, rain pouring down on him, the butt sponge-like as it fought the match.

He had won that struggle, his eight-year-old cupped hands circled in victory, lungs inhaling, body waiting for all that had been promised.

He thought of other times, blue smoke curling above a pool table, a bit of money in his pocket, youth holding his head high, able to see the balls go in pockets before he shot. Seeing it with the clear blue certainty of the chalked pool cue, seeing everything before him, knowing everything, then suddenly one day being on the other side of all of it.

He put the cigarette in his shirt pocket, closing his eyes to other tobacco memories. The thrill of a boy sharing his cigarette with a girl, his lips touching the moist paper that her lips had just left, the red-tasting lipstick thrilling him even as she walked away and never had a thought of him again. He had loved her for that, and wanted her always.

And the shared acrid smoke of all the times after all the love with Michaela. He pushed that away. He pushed away everything about her because he had to.

Now he had the wrapped promise in both hands. He sat on the floor, knees up close to his face as he inhaled the tobacco fragrance of his hands and the memories of every cigarette he ever smoked.

She knows I love her. She knows it. She knows that and she understands. She will understand, she will, and now I must not think of that. I must recall the first time I drove a car, the window open, that cigarette dangling on my lips as I turned that wheel to make the world go this way and that.

The sun rose through a yellow watery sky, moved higher to burn off all rival colors, holding the Lower Falls close in its white gaze. Shadows were squeezed tight, furtive beneath moving feet, as the faded paint and sharp cracks of myriad walls elbowed to the fore.

It was jarring how a week without rain changed the texture of the streets. Now just after mid-day the place took on the air of another country. A foreign place where things had become bleached by sunlight, where dust hovered over life and the natives knew that refuse brought by the wind would, in God's good time, be taken away by the same dry breezes.

Sound too was sharper today, crackling up and down sidewalks, carrying easily over roofs. The local pavement sent out its messages and received them from other places. Mothers called out to young sons and were answered by other mothers, unseen and calling a separate brood. Through these noises the voices of the boys were background—assuring, denying, pleading that they would be just a minute, bolstering their case with the familiar names of playmates.

Beyond these soft noises, the soldiers within the confines of their Saracen bounced and tilted with the contours of the city terrain. They seemed a seated chorus line, bowing and tilting, sliding left and right behind their rifles.

Three of their number peered straight ahead—the driver, his seatmate and their sergeant, glaring back at the sunlight— watching, watching at what this hostile world would hurl at them next. A fourth soldier stared out a rear view slit, seeing

Irish people fade to specks as others slid into view, all pretending not to see the armored car.

Those who thought they recognized the man walking up the street's long incline blinked in uncertainty. That pause made quick room for the rumble of the English machine, turning off Falls Road onto Leeson Street, where pedestrians thought only of safety as the Saracen came toward them, or felt a chill on the neck as the machine rumbled up from behind. The man stepped off the curb and into the street.

Jimmy Fitzgerald felt the refreshing embrace of comfort. He could not remember when he had felt it last. The easy hold of who he was, the sureness that his name was his own, his fate in his hands, the freedom of it pouring over him and spilling around his feet. His hands too felt the coolness of certainty, something he could feel growing, feel lifting him as he moved, all the dirt from within dissolving, his knowledge now coming clean and quick.

Something about the pedestrian caught the attention of Sergeant David Nathan. The walking man was too sure, his gaze too steady and he was looking right at the Saracen grinding toward him.

"Watch it," the sergeant said to his driver, squeezing the man's shoulder for emphasis.

Like photographers peering into a lens, the soldiers turned, keeping the jostling image of Jimmy in the center of the view slit. They saw him grow larger as he strode and the machine swept down on him.

"Watch him lads, watch him."

Safeties clicked off rifles and the driver twice cleared his throat.

Mary Burke saw the drama, immediately recognized who the man in the middle of the street was and crossed herself, stepping back against a wall.

Liz Moran saw too, whispering to God, the cigarette

abruptly halting in its journey to her mouth. Liz saw the Saracen making Jimmy smaller and smaller as she hoarsely whispered,

"Get away, Jimmy, get away."

With the distance at seventy-five feet Jimmy Fitzgerald, his shirt tucked in neatly, the soft breeze just lifting the hair on one side of his head, drew a pistol from the small of his back. In his vision the gun was blurred and black, floating, its barrel dipping left then right, while the Saracen snapped into sharp focus. He whispered Michaela's name, then the names of all the bartered dead.

"Fire, dammit, fire!" screamed the sergeant.

Jimmy fired first, the slug hitting the iron above the view slit. Firing again, he sent a round through the view slit. It careened off the ceiling and dug into a trooper's leg. His third shot was answered by an explosion of British fire, the driver screaming, his companions lurching forward—cursing, jamming rifle barrels into the slit, loosing a sea of shouts and bullets.

Jimmy fired again, this shot banging into the front of the Saracen as he was smashed off his feet and hurled backwards. The soldiers kept firing as their vehicle careened past him, jumped the curb and gouged a wall.

Throwing open the rear doors the British leapt out, flame bearers, as their rifles roared at the inert form in the middle of the street.

"Cease fire! Cease fire!"

Their sergeant's voice corralled their rage, allowing them to replace thunderous gunfire with silent kicks. This too the sergeant ordered stopped, and they stood in a circle, gasping, shocked at what they had done and what had almost been done to them. The soldiers' hands shook as they reached to click on the safeties of their rifles, responding to shouted commands to spread out, to watch the roofs, the windows, the doorways, the Irish.

Clutching the radio at his chest, Sergeant Davis quietly called for reinforcements as a crowd poured around them. The sergeant had seen this before. Those moments of shock when uniforms and nationality mean nothing. When both sides stand mute at the carnage, not soldiers or citizens, but temporarily just people trying to comprehend the sudden ending of young life.

The veteran sergeant saw something else. Saw not just the usual shock, but quiet disbelief. He saw them looking at one another, not speaking but saying something with their eyes. It was not that they couldn't believe the soldiers had killed, it was *who* they had killed that had them all silent.

The people were confused. They saw the pistol, the dead man, the soldiers, but they were not coming to their usual instant violent conclusion. Rather, the sergeant saw, they were trying to understand, to fit this thing into their universe. Something, Sergeant Davis saw, was out of balance here.

More soldiers arrived, but the crowd didn't move, didn't go for paving stones or bottles, they just stared. Hours later people were still staring, coming in twos and threes to look at the spot, to point and retrace the journey of the Saracen, and the blood stained spot where the man made his stand. In their minds the men all saw themselves in his place, and they shivered at the thought. Imagine, they whispered. Imagine the courage. Then they went away, and others came to point, to picture the thing, to touch the spots where the fusillade had hit walls and pavement, where the machine had met the wall. They kept coming even in the dark, until word was given that they were not to come, that there were to be no mementoes placed, no public speculation made, no conclusion reached.

Ian MacDonald felt something pull his glance to the telephone and then the device rang. It was the young detective Bell, the one who had been at the scene of the soldiers killed inside their armored car.

Could Detective MacDonald come straight away? An urgent matter, thank you, Sir.

Now as he rocked inside the Saracen, he felt the eyes of the soldiers on the opposite bench upon him. He heard the sharp smash of a bottle overhead, the ping of rocks hitting armor, the fleeting shouted insults over the engine noise.

Then the vehicle stopped, the rear doors were shoved open, to frame a dun colored blanket. The blanket only hinted at what was beneath, a slight rise at one end, gentle slopes. But the pavement spoke aloud, its surface displaying a crimson stream with myriad tiny red tributaries.

Bell greeted MacDonald in a whisper.

"Didn't want to say too much over the phone, Sir."

MacDonald nodded his understanding as Bell stepped over to the blanket, crouching, slowly pulling it back.

The blanket bent to reveal face, chest, stomach.

MacDonald grimaced.

"Eleven wounds, Sir, pretty much point-blank."

Bell stood, to whisper, "But the thing, Sir, the reason I called you."

He slid the blanket back over the body, then motioned MacDonald closer. The two men crouched as Bell took Jimmy's hand and turned it palm upward.

In blue ink MacDonald's private phone line stared back at him. Bell tucked the hand back under the blanket.

"Thought I should contact you."

"Bell."

"Yes, Sir?"

"Has anyone else seen this?"

"No, Sir."

MacDonald felt like a hunter who stumbles upon a flock of birds that explodes from the underbrush. He was startled, there were targets, but there was very little time.

"You've done good work, in fact excellent work. And I won't forget that."

"Yes, Sir."

Getting a canteen from the Saracen MacDonald wet a handkerchief and then gently rubbed the number off the cool skin.

He told Bell to file a report that did not mention the phone number. He spoke to the soldiers, taking notes of each man's words. Their descriptions were nearly verbatim. The man in the street growing larger and larger then suddenly pulling out a pistol. Their ears still ringing from the answering of their rifles, the feet going up, they all remembered that. The flash of the soles of his shoes as he arched backwards.

Then it was on to the morgue where, after the doctor had left the room, MacDonald stood alone reading reports. As alone that was, as one can be with the newly dead. The dead you had spoken to, touched, with whom you had matched wits. Every word he read seemed accompanied by Jimmy's voice, by Jimmy's presence above and just behind MacDonald's neck. He felt a chill.

The attendant entered the room, the two men nodded and MacDonald left for his office so as to stay close to his phone, his desk, his power. He wrote a brief, bland report and just after sunset, turned off the lights. Striding toward his car he glanced at the strings of barbed wire encircling this place, at the sandbags protecting and simultaneously pressing everything into the earth with tons of muffled resentment.

Inside the car he glanced at the passenger seat, picturing Jimmy there, but he pushed that away. He put the key in the ignition, the key slipping, not quite meshing with the slot, he pushed harder, now the key was vibrating in his hand.

Ian MacDonald saw Jimmy's face, Jimmy's wounds, Jimmy's lungs flat and still, the way his own lungs felt now with this sudden hammering of his heart.

He tried to draw air, heard his rasping breath, felt his heart trying to tear loose from its seat in his chest.

Breathe, he told himself, *breathe*, but the air wasn't coming in, he was suffocating with a hundred gasps, now sweat covered him, as he slid within his clothing.

I'm dying, having a heart attack, suffocating, I'm dying.

Panic grabbed him, he fumbled with the door handle, staggered out, cool night air over him, his chest being crushed, shaking soaked in perspiration, he grabbed the car's roof.

That's better, the cool air, holding the roof, there now, I can breathe, heart slowing, yes, air in air out, yes, focus boy focus, stay upright, breathe breathe.

He pulled his coat off, shoved it inside, wiping his face with one arm. *God what was all that?* He looked around, saw no one watching then slid behind the steering wheel. He took a slow deep breath, *I'm fine, I'm fine,* and he was suddenly crying.

He couldn't stop, tried to regain control, only to gasp, cry louder and then cry more. He didn't know why he was weeping, nor from where inside him, this outburst sprang. Minutes passed, how many, three, five, ten? He had no idea but finally it left him. He was ashamed, frightened, angry at nothing, afraid of the whole world at once.

With both hands Ian MacDonald managed to get the key into the ignition, to turn the wheel, to not drive into the metal gate before the soldiers had opened it.

Then home, to family, to surprisingly swift sleep, swift but without dreams, bereft of succor, the emptiness relentlessly pulling, pulling him to daylight.

Days passed, the detective working his sources with the growing sense that he was laboring at a well gone dry. MacDonald glided again within his routine of homecoming, his pattern of trying to avoid the usual, as in an ever tighter circle he coasted toward what was most familiar. His gaze swept streets, sidewalks, rooftops and corners. Reversing direction, he repeated a rough circumference of his neighborhood, moving toward the calm family harbor that allowed him to face the day after this.

Nothing looked different—an old man walking his little dog, a woman bundled and bent, pushing a baby's pram. All was normal, all was as expected, and for that reason the detective slid the car into another gear and resumed his elliptical wanderings.

He focused on the man and his dog, the man's belly over his trousers, the dog's delight at this whiff of freedom, this hint of the hunt for which his breed was created. In the rearview mirror he watched the young mother, observed the large white wheels and the woman's complete focus on the pram's precious contents. Then MacDonald turned off that avenue and onto the little dead end street of his home.

He stopped, noting the curtain move, the hand of his wife there, then the peeping out of a smiling little boy. The policeman smiled, kept his hand on his revolver but smiled, and he saw his wife smiling. He dared think, *someday, all this will end and they will come out to hug me. And we will have won, we will have defeated evil and I will stand in this street without a weapon.*

I will put my arms around my wife and son and hold them close, as close as love can hold anyone and we will be free.

He paused before shutting off the engine, waited for the slightest ruffle, the least bit of disturbance, and he saw there was nothing but his street, his home, his wife and little boy. Turning off the engine the detective saw the delighted little white dog leading the old man and felt reassurance at such a familiar sight. Getting out of the vehicle he thought of his little boy, of what wonders the child had discovered this day.

As he walked toward the front door he again glimpsed the woman pushing the pram on the return part of her journey. He looked at the faces in the window, saw his wife's smile, saw it freeze, and he saw the abandoned pram rolling, the woman running, running, running at him, fumbling in her loose clothing, the hand coming out, the heavy pistol pulling at it, the runner almost stumbling. But Louis did not stumble, did not hesitate as the policeman went for his revolver, and Louis's strides ate up the distance.

MacDonald's mind shouted *my wife! my child! my child! my child!* as his limbs went cold, his heart hot, and his arm came up, his eyes focusing on the running figure, the size of the running figure exploding in his sight.

The two men fired almost at once. Almost. Louis shot first, the shot hitting the other man, the man slumping into the side of the car. MacDonald felt the sledge hammer blow of the slug, disbelieving it had hit him even as the second bullet ripped deeply into him and set screaming parts of his body he had not known existed.

Louis ran and fired again, this bullet crumpling the man, as Louis's momentum carried him past the fallen detective.

The policeman was on the pavement—enraged, disbelieving, his body ignoring his commands, the pistol dropping from his numb hand. He stared at the weapon, willing his arm to obey, to pick it up. He stared, now almost detached as the light dimmed, two black curtains slowly sliding across his vision, closing, closing from both sides, almost meeting, but still that dim light held.

My wife, my boy, my boy, my boy. A man, this man dressed as a woman bending over me. Speaking, was he speaking to me? This darkness, this flowing away of the warmth enveloping me. What is he saying to me? Can't move, my wife, her voice is that her voice? Then two quick impacts, Ian MacDonald feeling himself jerk, hearing the reports of the pistol shots entering his chest. *The darkness now, this peace, this peace, yes, it is, it is, it is.*

Louis stood still as the screaming woman rushed past, he stood still to take in this place of privilege and orderliness. He saw the huffing old man and his wee yapping dog. Louis absorbed the faces at all the windows as the car screeched to a halt. He looked at this alien place again as the vehicle rushed him away, past the white dog, away from the spreading crimson on the clean sidewalk, away from this close-cropped order and toward the Lower Falls Road.

Sprawled in the back seat, he whispered the names of the dead, saw the driver turn and look at him, then Louis closed his eyes to see their faces and to repeat their names.

In the safe house he sat apart from the others, accepted a drink, nodded at their words, and sank deeper into himself. He felt no sense of accomplishment, no joy. He felt only time sweeping past, felt it as though the seconds were an elevator lowering him to the bosom of the planet. He felt everything coming down with him, then felt nothing but the rapid descent and the surrounding silence and the knowledge that he was completely alone. In this depth there was no struggle of nations, no comrades living or in patriot graves. There was, after all, only himself and the world. And, he understood, the world always wins.

Late the next night wind buffeted the hair of the man with the pistol, snapped the cuffs of his pants as he bent with the weapon. Gently placing it where Jimmy had fallen, he touched the weapon with the outstretched fingers of both hands, then slowly straightened, his form flowing into a salute. He stood for long moments, resolute as the crisp air, then very slowly his right arm came down to his side.

The others stared at the weapon that had killed the detective, glanced at one another, and then fell in step behind their commander, who led them back to small rooms and revolution. A few people saw, and Louis knew a few would be enough, knew that one would have been enough. Now they would all know, and the Smith & Wesson would be left untouched until the British Army found it.

In the past weeks she had shed her exhaustion with her tears, lost all fear, all rage, all thoughts of what might have been. Then she had returned to stand alone in the dark at the place her love had fallen.

She searched for a sign of the man who had been. She looked up and down the street, her glance settling upon the pockmarks on the wall. She couldn't focus enough to count them all, but they reassured her, told her that Jimmy's and her time together had been in a certain place and time and no one could take that, not ever. Then she simply stood.

Furtive footsteps came and went, the sounds of men and women alone and in small knots. It was the women who recognized her, the women whose voices fell silent only to burst into staccato whispers on the far curb. That too gave her succor. It drew with the finest of points the new boundaries of who she had become.

Absorbing all there was to this small piece of her country, Michaela thought of her little flat. The Brits would have wrecked the place. Her clothing would be strewn about, food tossed from containers, pillows ripped open, the stuffing from chairs posing in obscene display. And worst of all they would have torn the pages of books, kicked the tomes and ground them on the floor. There would be solace in smoothing that paper, in rubbing an index finger along those lettered wounds. She could see the colors of all those titles, the rows of words.

And now she could feel a man standing near. She turned to see Louis Duffy, his features drawn hard and clear even in this

Falls Road darkness. Yards away loomed darker smudges on the night's canvas, where other men stood with the casual certainty of the armed. The woman, still looking at the wounded wall, spoke first.

"He died a man."

"Aye."

"As he lived."

"Aye."

The pair looked together at the wall with its echo of the brief struggle.

Louis asked, "You'll stay, then?"

"I'm home aren't I?"

She saw him nod in agreement.

"Michaela."

The woman focused her gaze on him.

"The Brits could make it awful hard on ye. An' some ones that live here, them ones could be bitter."

She nodded her head, the breeze pushing her hair forward to touch her face.

"There's nothing anyone can do to me."

Louis hesitated, his eyes absorbing the wall, the young woman, and the streets that met here.

"Michaela."

Taking her head in one hand he kissed her soft hair.

"Godspeed."

He stepped back, the soft layer of sand on concrete crunching as he turned. He went quickly into the gloom, the shadows of comrades moving with him, all vanishing, flickering into perception once more, all in motion, all gone.

CPSIA information can be obtained at www.ICGtesting.com
Printed in the USA
LVOW042136291112

309299LV00001B/1/P